Heartland

❧

Love Is a Gift

by Lauren Brooke

SCHOLASTIC INC.

New York Toronto London Auckland Sydney
Mexico City New Delhi Hong Kong Buenos Aires

With special thanks to Elisabeth Faith

*For Amber Caravéo — Thank you
for making Heartland a
special place.*

ISBN 0-439-42510-7

Heartland series created by Working Partners Limited, London.

Copyright © 2004 by Working Partners Ltd.
Published by Scholastic Inc. All rights reserved.

12 11 10 9 8 7   7 8 9/0
Printed in the U.S.A.   40
First Scholastic printing, March 2004

Chapter One

❧

Amy threw the lead rope down on the floor in exasperation. "I don't know what's gotten into him!" she exclaimed. The stallion careered around the paddock with his tail kinked in the air like a banner. Amy glanced across at Ty who was leaning against the fence post, watching. Ty tried to look sympathetic, but Amy could see that he was smiling. She made a mock scowl at her boyfriend. "You know, you're not helping matters."

"I'm sorry," Ty apologized, trying to suppress his grin. "It's just that Dazzle looks like he's having a lot of fun. He probably thinks you're playing tag!"

Amy shook her head and felt a corresponding bubble of laughter well up inside her. She thought about how nice it was to have Ty back at Heartland. It was not long

1

ago that he had been in the hospital in a coma. Those weeks had been devastating for Amy. Ty was so much more than just the lead stable hand at Heartland. He was her best friend and boyfriend. She pushed a stray strand of hair away from her face as she joined him at the fence.

As soon as Amy stopped pursuing Dazzle, the stallion halted his exuberant gallop. Now the mustang was watching Amy and Ty with his ears pricked forward in interest.

"Hey." Ty snapped his fingers. "Earth to Amy."

Amy looked up at Ty and smiled warmly. "I was just thinking about how good it is to have you home," she said.

"It's nice to know you missed me," Ty replied, smiling back as he went and scooped up the rope from the floor. "Want me to give it a try?"

Amy nodded and watched as Ty quietly approached Dazzle with the rope behind his back. The mustang stood in the center of the paddock, following Ty's every movement. Just as Ty drew close enough to reach out his hand, Dazzle let out a high-pitched squeal and wheeled away. Instead of chasing after the blue roan, Ty immediately turned his back and showed no interest in Dazzle's antics. The stallion bucked several times in high spirits, but Ty resolutely ignored him. Gradually, the mustang began to calm down.

Seeing the puzzled expression on Dazzle's face as he

looked at Ty made Amy smile. The mustang eventually lowered his head, snorted heavily, and made his way over to nuzzle Ty's shoulder. He snorted once more as Ty slowly turned and clipped on his lead rope to walk him to the gate.

"He still responds better to you than to anyone else," Amy commented as they walked into the coolness of the barn. There was a full hay net hanging in the corner of the stall, thoughtfully left there by Ben, the other stable hand at Heartland.

"He'd just tired himself out and was finally ready to come in," Ty replied, slipping off Dazzle's head collar.

But Amy knew that there was an extra-special bond between Ty and the mustang. "Ben's already prepared the feed buckets, so we just have to take them to the stalls and we're done," she declared.

Ty straightened up. "Terrific," he replied.

Just then they heard Lou, Amy's sister, calling from the house. "Amy, can you come in when you've got a second?"

"Go ahead," Ty told Amy. "I'll finish up here. There's not much left to do."

"Are you sure?" Amy frowned. She didn't want Ty to overdo things so soon after his time in the hospital.

"Go on. It might be important," he said, leaning forward to kiss Amy on the forehead. "I'll see you in the morning."

"Thanks, Ty," Amy said gratefully, and patted Dazzle before slipping from the stall.

❧

Lou and Scott were sitting at the kitchen table with Jack Bartlett, the girls' grandfather. Amy kicked off her shoes as she walked in and noted with surprise that her sister did not instinctively tell her to put them in the closet, "where they belong."

Amy smiled a welcome to Scott, Lou's boyfriend and the vet for Heartland. He and Lou had been dating for a while now. She glanced at Lou sitting alongside him and immediately noticed an air of excitement surrounding her normally calm sister. She realized they were all regarding her with steady gazes. "What's happening?" Amy asked curiously.

"Well," Lou began, giving Scott a quick glance, "I was wondering, do you think you could manage without me for a couple of weeks?" Her blue eyes shone as she reached across the table to put her hand over Scott's. "Scott is flying to Australia for a conference in about two weeks — and he wants me to go with him. He bought me a ticket and everything."

"For a couple of weeks!" Amy exclaimed in surprise.

"Well, it might be a little more than that by the time you add in the travel," Lou admitted. "The conference lasts for five days, but since it's in Australia I thought we might visit Daddy. I called him today and he's invited me to stay with him, Helena, and the baby while Scott is at the conference. Then, when Scott's free, we thought we'd take a quick vacation together before heading home," she explained, excitement in her voice.

Thoughts raced through Amy's mind. After their mom had died, Lou had given up her banking job in the city and moved to Heartland to take over the business side of things, which made it possible for Amy to continue their mother's work of caring for abused and neglected horses. The thought of her sister being gone for an extended period suddenly made Amy realize just how big a part of Heartland Lou had become.

"Amy?" Lou prompted gently. Amy looked up and could tell by the way the excitement had left her sister's eyes that a pensive silence wasn't the reaction Lou had been hoping for.

Amy took a deep breath and forced herself to smile. "That's great news, Lou. Of course you should go. You deserve a break after all the hard work you've done. And how many chances will you get to visit Dad?"

Lou looked delighted. She pushed back her chair and hurried around the table to give Amy a hug. "Are you sure you can spare me?"

Amy pushed down the mixed feelings that were whirling around in her stomach and hugged her sister back. "Sure, I'm sure."

Scott cleared his throat and said, "I've arranged for a vet with a very good reputation to cover for me and look after the practice while we're away."

Amy smiled across at him as Lou added, "And I'll make sure all the paperwork's completely up-to-date. You shouldn't have too much to do while I'm away. You'll just have to remember to pay all the bills at the end of the month, check our e-mail every day, and —"

"Enough, enough," Jack broke in, laughing. "I'm sure you'll leave detailed instructions for everything — and instructions on how to follow the instructions! Amy, I'll cover most of Lou's work for her. You have enough to do as it is."

"Thanks, Grandpa. I'm sure we'll manage," Amy replied.

"That's terrific," said Lou. "I'll call Daddy back and say yes to his invitation. Thanks so much, Amy, Grandpa." She looked from one to the other. "You have no idea what this means to me. "

Amy had been so focused on Lou's being away that it hadn't sunk in that her sister would be spending a fair amount of time with their father in Australia — time she would have loved to share with them. It was difficult not to envy Lou's opportunity. As Lou began to punch their father's number into the phone, Amy quietly slid her feet into her boots and slipped back outside.

When Amy let herself into Sundance's stall, her pony

looked up from his hay net and nickered softly. "Oh, Sundance," Amy whispered, tangling her fingers in his mane. She leaned against his warm golden neck as familiar feelings of loss swept over her. She was happy that Lou was going to Australia. Her sister deserved a vacation, and Amy knew how much the chance to spend time with their father would mean to her. But somehow Lou's announcement had disturbed the strong sense of family and security that Amy had grown to rely on since her mother's death. Amy wasn't sure why Lou's going away made her feel uneasy.

She gave a deep sigh. *Whenever I think I'm handling things and am ready to move on, something happens that makes all the doubt return, the sense that something is still missing.* Sundance's ears flickered toward Amy. He turned his head and lipped gently at her hair. Amy leaned against the pony, drawing comfort from his warmth and strength.

"I thought I might find you here," Jack said quietly, glancing over the stall door. "You always come out to the horses when you have some thinking to do."

Amy turned to look at her grandfather.

"What's on your mind?" he asked, his blue eyes showing concern.

Amy hesitated and straightened Sundance's forelock. "I guess I'm not a hundred percent sure how I feel about Lou leaving," she admitted.

"You wish you were going, too?" Jack inquired sympathetically.

Amy patted Sundance's shoulder before joining her grandfather at the door. "I would love to see Dad again," she agreed. "But more than that, I've suddenly realized how much I've come to need Lou. How much her being here makes us feel like a real family."

"I know," Jack said, and squeezed her arm reassuringly. "And I bet Lou would appreciate hearing that. You should go and talk to her."

❧

Lou looked up from where she was rinsing cups at the sink as Amy opened the kitchen door.

"Did Scott leave?" Amy asked.

"Yes, he has a lot to do before our trip," Lou replied as she wiped her hands dry. "But I'm glad we've got a minute to talk. I want to make sure that you really are OK about this trip, now that you've had a chance to think about it. Earlier, I had the feeling that you weren't all that open about how you felt. I know it's kind of sudden."

"I'm thrilled for you," Amy reassured her quickly. "It's just that it won't seem so much like home with you gone. And I know it's selfish, but I really wish I could go, too. I'd love to see Dad."

Lou looked a little shaken. "I was worried you might feel like that," she said quietly.

"No, I don't want you to worry," Amy continued, pulling out a chair and sitting down at the table. "I think it's great that you're getting this chance to go — I really do. What did Dad say when you spoke to him?"

"He was pleased," Lou replied, joining Amy at the table. "He said he'd call me soon to finalize the arrangements — and he sent you his love."

Amy smiled. It was only recently that she had begun to get to know her father, Tim Fleming. When Amy was only three, he had been traumatized by a bad show-jumping accident — and had abandoned his family when he thought he would never ride again. Amy and Lou had not seen their father for twelve years — until a couple of months ago. During his brief stay at Heartland, Amy and her father had, to her surprise, bonded well. Lou, being older, had had more time to develop a close relationship with their father before his accident, yet she had found it harder to find common ground with Tim. Amy hoped that *this* trip would give Lou the chance to regain the closeness she had shared with her father in her childhood. Since Tim now lived in Australia with his new wife and daughter, Amy and Lou didn't have many opportunities to spend time with him, and they hadn't yet met Tim's wife, Helena.

"Why don't you take some photos of yourself and the rest of us working at Heartland?" Lou suggested. "Then I can take them with me. I'll make sure I take lots of photos when I'm at Dad's ranch — of him and Helena and their baby, Lily. I know it won't be the same, but . . ." Her voice trailed off helplessly.

"That's a great idea," said Amy quickly. She grinned. "They can see what's happening here. And I know you'll be sure to take photos of every single one of Dad's horses just for me, won't you?"

"Of course," Lou nodded, smiling back. "We wouldn't want you to miss out on the really important aspect of the trip!"

❧

Early the next morning, Amy pulled on her clothes and headed out to feed the horses. She was just mixing the last bucket when Ty arrived. "You must have been up even earlier than usual," he commented, glancing at his watch.

"I didn't sleep much," Amy replied.

"That seems to be a trend lately." Ty frowned. "You're going to wear yourself out, keeping such long hours."

Amy looked away, not wanting to catch his eye. The truth was that she had been trying to take on more of the stable chores in an attempt to lighten Ty's workload. Amy didn't want Ty to push himself too hard. But Amy knew that Ty was too proud to accept help, so she didn't want to draw attention to her efforts. Quickly changing the subject, she brought Ty up-to-date with Lou's news from the previous evening. Ty agreed that sending photos of Heartland to Tim was a good idea.

"I thought I'd take a few shots of Sundance and Sugarfoot and then some of you and Ben turning horses out in the paddocks," Amy told him, grabbing buckets of grain as she spoke.

Ben's horse, Red, was looking over his stable door, eagerly anticipating his morning feed. "Then if you could take some of me working with Dazzle in the ring," she went on, giving Red a pat, "it will give Helena a good idea of what goes on during a typical day at Heartland."

"Is there such a thing?" Ty joked, picking up a grooming kit.

"Good morning!" Ben called as he arrived on the yard.

"Hi, Ben," Ty called. Then he looked back at Amy. "I'd better get going. We want all the horses looking their best for their Australian cousins, don't we?"

"Australia? Have I missed something?" Ben asked, looking confused.

"A lot!" Amy laughed. "If you want an update, you can come along. I've got some photos to take, and you can be my model."

❧

After Amy had taken photos of Ben and Ty doing the morning chores, Ty took the camera as Amy led Dazzle into the ring. Dazzle was a mustang stallion that had come to Heartland while Ty was still in the hospital. Amy had had difficulty connecting with the stallion. He was wild and proud, and he had never interacted with people. But when Ty had come back to Heartland while he was recovering, he was able to develop a bond with Dazzle. Since the stallion had responded so quickly to Ty, Amy had suggested that he be the one to handle the training of the mustang.

Now Amy was beginning to do more work with Dazzle herself. "Here we go, boy," she said, stopping in the middle of the ring and unclipping the lead rein. Dazzle snorted loudly as she drove him away from her to the outside of the ring and then sent him cantering freely around the perimeter. Amy knew it wouldn't be long before the stallion showed signs of wanting to join up with her. She was gradually gaining his trust now, and she knew that each time they completed a join up, the bond between them grew. Watching the stallion eat up the ground with his long stride, his tail streaming out behind him, Amy felt a rush of pride. She forgot about Ty and the photos; all her concentration was focused on the beautiful stallion that was now asking to join up with her. He had lowered his head and was opening and closing his mouth, waiting for Amy to allow him to cross the ring and be with her.

Amy deliberately dropped her aggressive stance, turned her body sideways to the horse, and waited. Dazzle slowed to a stop, and Amy could sense him watching her. The hairs on the back of her neck tingled as she waited for him to approach. Slowly, Dazzle crossed the ring and came to a halt beside Amy, blowing deeply on her shoulder. Amy raised her hand and gently rubbed his nose. Then she took a few steps forward, and as if they were bound by an invisible thread, Dazzle followed her. Wherever Amy went, the mustang walked patiently behind, showing her the utmost trust and respect. "See, that wasn't so bad, was it?" she said, running her fingers through the horse's mane. "You were just feeling spunky yesterday, weren't you?"

With the session ended, Ty walked over and snapped Dazzle's lead rein back on. "He's really beginning to respond to you," Ty enthused, leading Dazzle out of the ring. "I think I got some great pictures. Looking at him now, there's no way anyone would guess how wild and defiant he was when he arrived."

Amy nodded and patted Dazzle's warm neck. "He still has a way to go, but he's coming along well. And most of that's because of you," she added. Then she glanced across at Ty and noticed that his face looked pale, his expression blank. "Are you OK?" she asked anxiously.

"Sure," Ty replied. "Don't worry so much. I'm fine."

"Well, you look tired," said Amy stubbornly. "You should take a break. I'll rub Dazzle down."

"Trust me, I'm OK," Ty insisted, and clicked to Dazzle to follow him into the barn.

"Ty," Amy called after him, but he didn't turn back. Amy sighed. He was determined to do everything for himself, she realized. From now on, when she was trying to help, she'd have to be even less obvious about it.

❧

The next week was filled with Lou's preparations to leave. Despite Amy's and Grandpa's constant reassurances that they knew what to do in her absence, Lou was determined to leave Heartland as well organized as possible.

Amy was busy sweeping the yard when she heard the kitchen door fly open. Looking up, she saw Lou rushing toward her, flapping a large white envelope.

"Look at this," Lou yelled, still strides away. "It's for you. I think it's from Dad." Amy stared in surprise at her sister's enthusiasm.

Puzzled, Amy took the envelope and opened it. Her gray eyes widened as she scanned the letter. "You're right, it is from Dad," she said slowly. "He wants me to come to Australia with you and Scott! Did you know about this?"

"No," Lou gasped. "He didn't say anything about it to

me. He must have wanted it to be a surprise," she said in delight.

Amy reread the letter — more carefully this time.

Dear Amy,

I know that by now Lou will have told you of her plans to come to Australia. The time that you and I spent together at Heartland was very special, and it would mean a great deal to me if you could come with Lou. We could spend longer with each other this time — our last visit was too short. Helena says she looks forward to getting to know you both — and introducing you to your younger sister, of course! I know that it won't be easy for you to leave Heartland, but promise you'll try to come. I want to show you my current stock of horses, and I have told everyone here about your special touch. I won't be the only one disappointed if you don't make it!

Please give my regards to Jack, and tell Lou that we are looking forward to seeing her and Scott. I'm also looking forward to taking a ride with her — I know she's been practicing since my last visit! I'm enclosing a plane ticket for you and hope you will be able to use it. All my love,
Daddy

"This is wonderful!" Lou's eyes shone. "You'll love being at Daddy's ranch — spending time with him and seeing all his horses. And we can get to know our sister together."

Her voice trailed off as Amy looked up, slowly shaking her head. "It's no good, Lou. We can't both leave Heartland. I just can't go."

Chapter Two

꩜

Amy slid the halter farther over her shoulder as she walked down to the paddock with her best friend, Soraya. Even the sight of Sundance standing at the gate did little to lift her spirits.

"Amy, why are you so set against going?" Soraya questioned. "I know you'd love to see your dad's ranch. Come on. Why don't you at least try to figure out a way you could go?"

"There's just no point." Amy sighed, pushing a strand of hair out of her eyes. "I couldn't leave Ty and Ben to do all the work on their own. I mean, Grandpa's going to be busy enough with his and Lou's share."

Soraya flipped her black curly hair over her shoulder and walked across to Jasmine, one of the long-term residents at Heartland. Jasmine was an ex-dressage pony

17

that had been about to be put down due to habitual lameness when Amy's mom rescued her. With treatment and care, Amy's mom had restored Jasmine's soundness so she could be used for light work. Soraya buckled a halter on the pretty, dish-faced pony and led her to fall into step beside Amy and Sundance. The buckskin pony swished his tail in annoyance and laid his ears back, rolling the whites of his eyes dramatically.

"You stop it!" said Amy. For once Sundance's bad-tempered antics failed to amuse her. Sundance was so clearly surprised at being scolded by Amy that he lowered his head and walked quietly beside her.

Soraya laughed. "I've never seen Sundance so well behaved," she said. "Perhaps you should yell at him more often."

Amy immediately felt awful. "Sorry, boy, I'm just a little stressed," she murmured, patting his neck. Sundance snorted and gave her a sharp nudge with his nose that made her smile.

Once they had tacked up and were clattering out of the yard toward the sandy track that would take them up Teak's Hill, Amy felt her spirits lift. It seemed as if Sundance sensed her foul mood for he did everything with more enthusiasm than usual, as if he was trying to cheer her up. He galloped faster, jumped higher, and felt lighter than ever before.

"Wow!" Soraya gasped as they pulled up for a rest.

"What's gotten into him? The way he cleared that fallen tree should qualify him for the Olympic trials!"

Amy grinned, and as they headed for home she began to think over Soraya's earlier suggestion of finding a way to go to Australia. After riding in silence for a while, she turned to her friend. "I just don't see how they could manage all the work without me for so long. A week, yes, but not two. It just wouldn't be fair. We can't afford to hire a temporary stable hand, and Ty still needs to take things easy after his accident. There's no way he could take on my work on top of what he's doing already."

"I wouldn't mind coming and helping for a couple of hours each day," Soraya offered generously. "With play practice over, I have a lot of extra time."

Amy considered her offer for a moment before shaking her head regretfully. "Thanks, that's really kind of you, but there's just so much to do. Morning feeds, turning out, exercising, working with the horses, mucking out the stalls, evening feeds, and then trying to keep the yard clean." She looked across at her friend and grinned. "Wow, I didn't realize how hard I work."

Soraya smiled in return. "I know I couldn't put in the hours that you do, but I'd still be able to take on some of the stable work. If you ask me, you need a vacation — particularly with everything you've been through lately."

Amy sank into thought. The last few months had been pretty tough, with the equine flu that put Heartland under quarantine and the tornado that had ripped through the farm and caused Ty's accident. "I would love to go," she admitted to her friend. "But Heartland comes first," she added firmly.

"I know." Soraya nodded her head, looking serious. "But I think it's time you admitted that the problem isn't really how we would all cope without you but how you would cope without us!" She broke into a wide grin as Amy pretended to take a swat at her, before shortening her reins and cantering back to the yard.

✥

After cooling the horses and then going inside for hot chocolate, Amy waved Soraya off. As she turned to walk back to the farmhouse, she saw Ty, Ben, Lou, and Grandpa all huddled together in the yard. Amy raised her eyebrows questioningly at Ty.

"We've been talking, and we've decided that you should go to Australia," he announced, getting straight to the point.

Amy sighed. "Yeah, I'd love to go, but it's just not fair. It's too much work for you three to manage on your own."

Ben stepped forward and Amy could see concern in his eyes. "Spending some time with your dad and his new family is too important for anything else to get in the way, Amy — even Heartland." Amy knew where he was coming from. Ben took family matters seriously. He had had a strained relationship with his mother for years, and he was talking from hard experience.

"I know, Ben," she said, biting her lip. "But — "

"How would you feel if we could get someone else to work here while you're away?" Lou interrupted. "And let's say this person is familiar with Heartland and would do the work for free."

Amy looked from one face to the next and suddenly realized that they all knew something she didn't. She thought quickly, and then her gray eyes widened with excitement. "Marnie!" she said.

Lou nodded, her blue eyes dancing.

"But for two whole weeks?" she questioned. Amy knew Marnie well. She and Lou had been good friends in New York, and she often came to help out as a reprieve from city life.

"I was talking with her about a month ago," Lou said, "and she mentioned that her job was really getting to her. She was thinking of putting in for a leave of absence just to get away from it all for a while. I suddenly realized this morning that she might like the idea of coming to stay here. She's always loved helping out, and she knows the stable routine. So I called her while you were out riding and she jumped at the chance," Lou explained. "At least think about it, Amy," she urged.

Just for a moment, Amy felt excitement well up inside her at the thought of going to Australia. "I'll consider it," she said, and before anyone could say any more, she stepped away and headed toward the tack room. She felt so torn. She would love to go to Australia with Lou, but she knew that she would worry about Ty and Heartland and that could end up spoiling her stay, which wouldn't be fair to Lou or her father.

❧

"Hey," Ty's voice broke into Amy's thoughts. She gave him a quick smile and returned her attention to the bridle she was adjusting. He sat down beside her on a storage trunk. "You know you'll regret it if you don't go," he pointed out.

"I've thought it through," said Amy quietly. "And it's not just the extra work you would all have to do if I wasn't here. I'm also worried that I might get in the way of Dad and Lou."

"What?" Ty looked puzzled.

"The last time Dad visited, I got to spend a lot of time with him and work through a lot of my issues. But Lou didn't really get close to him — not like she'd hoped. I think that if they have this time together in Australia, she'll be able to build a better relationship with him."

Amy knew that their shared love of horses had helped her and her father rebuild their relationship, but it had not been as easy for Lou. Lou was twelve at the time of Tim's accident, and it left her with a profound fear of horses. Though she had been an accomplished rider, she did not ride after their father left the family. Amy remembered how she had come to realize why Lou had skirted the Heartland stables and refused to ride. It had only been recently that her sister had started to enjoy being around horses again. Now there wasn't anything that would hinder Lou from feeling close to their father.

"Amy, you're not allowing yourself to see the whole picture," Ty replied gently. "All you've done is worry about the horses, worry about me, Lou, and your father. You should take a good look at all the good it'll do if you go."

Amy stared at him.

"I don't want you to stay because of me. Don't think I haven't noticed that you've been doing half my work for me," Ty continued. "It's time you let me get back into it. You have to trust my judgment on this, Amy." He looked intently at her. "Now's a good time for you to go. Heartland's been quieter than usual. Things were slow after the storm, so there are fewer horses. Candy's ready to go, and Dazzle actually works better with me than he does with you."

Amy nodded. She knew it was true.

"We can manage here. It's important for you to spend time with your father and meet your other sister. Just think things through before you make up your mind, OK?"

Amy looked thoughtfully at Ty. Even though there were still dark circles under his eyes, his face had an old, familiar expression of determination. She knew he was right.

❧

Later that afternoon, Amy let herself into the kitchen where Lou, Jack, Ben, and Ty were sitting around the table. Lou looked up, with a hopeful expression in her eyes. "Well?" she asked.

Amy couldn't think of a single thing to say.

Grandpa laughed. "Now that Amy's had every sensible argument taken away from her, I'm starting to think she doesn't actually *want* to go to Australia," he teased.

"Are you kidding?" Amy exclaimed. "I mean, it's not like I won't miss you guys," she said, glancing across into Ty's green eyes. "And the horses especially," she added.

"Gee, thanks," Ben joked.

"You know what I mean," Amy told him, running one hand through her long brown hair. "But getting to see Daddy again, and check out his ranch? *And* work with all his horses? I mean, wow!"

"It's supposed to be a vacation," Ty reminded her

gently, and everyone laughed. Lou raised her voice above the noise, "So does this mean you're going?"

"Well, I'd feel awful letting that plane ticket go to waste!" Amy replied happily as Ty crossed over to where she stood and hugged her.

🐍

Lou chewed the end of her pencil and looked again at her notepad. "There's still a lot to organize before we leave tomorrow. Have you packed yet?"

Amy nodded. "All done." She had packed a large duffel bag the previous evening. "And I called Dad to tell him when we get in."

"What did he say?" Lou asked, looking up.

"He said that he'd pick us up at the airport. Actually, we didn't get the chance to say much; the baby was crying and it was difficult to talk."

"Lily," Lou corrected.

Amy didn't reply. It had felt weird talking to her father with his new daughter making her presence so loudly felt. She couldn't really get her head around the fact that their father had three daughters now. Even though they had been apart for most of her life, Amy still thought that it was just Lou and she who belonged to him.

Lou didn't seem to have any such hang-ups. "I can't wait to meet her," she enthused. "Just think, a new sister!"

"Half sister," Amy murmured.

Lou returned to her list, a frown creasing her forehead. "I've ordered the grain, the hay, paid this month's bills," she muttered, ticking things off on her list.

"We need the farrier to come and trim Sundance's and Dazzle's feet," Amy reminded her.

As Lou reached for the phone, Amy left the room, eager to get in a final join-up session with Dazzle.

❧

That evening, Grandpa cooked a farewell meal for them all. As Amy looked around the table at the people she loved, she realized that she couldn't have chosen a better way to spend her final evening at home. Her feelings of excitement seemed to be infectious. Everyone chatted noisily about the trip to Australia.

Later on, Amy walked with Ty to his truck. "I'm really going to miss you," she said quietly.

"Me, too," he replied, turning to her. "But it's not often that you'll get this kind of opportunity."

She thought of how he often looked pale at the end of the day, though he never complained. "You mean getting out of school for a week with permission?" she asked with a laugh.

Ty clearly had read what was really on her mind. "You'll never have fun if you spend all of your time worrying about things here," he told her gently, reaching out for her hand.

"I'm sorry," Amy smiled. "I just feel guilty about leaving when you need a vacation more than I do."

Ty started to give her a look of disapproval, but his eyes dropped to focus on her hand in his. "It'll be good. Everything will be fine, just as long as you promise to e-mail me," he said.

Amy laughed. "I promise," she replied. "Only if you promise to reply. You know I'll be curious about everything that's happening here."

"Oh, I know," Ty assured her. He bent down and kissed her gently and held her for a moment longer than usual before climbing into his truck.

As Amy watched the taillights disappearing down the drive, Lou called from the kitchen, interrupting her thoughts. "Amy, don't forget we have an early start tomorrow," she pointed out. And despite her worries, Amy couldn't help but feel a thrill of excitement.

❧

Amy's time in Australia would overlap the Presidents' Day break, and Grandpa had spoken with her teachers about her taking off an additional week. Amy would have to cart her textbooks with her on the plane, but she knew it was a small price to pay for a week free of classroom lectures. Despite her joke about school, Amy was still feeling anxious about the prospect of leaving Ty. She worried he would push himself too hard, trying to get more than his share of the work done.

Amy was up very early the next morning. She hadn't been able to sleep well. She was too excited. She pulled on her work clothes and hurried outside, intending to do as much as she could before leaving. Rising before it was even light also meant she would have some time on her own with the horses to say her good-byes.

First she decided to collect the hay nets from the stalls and fill them for the evening. She figured it would make Marnie's first day a little easier. As she walked toward the stable block, the horses stirred restlessly in their deep straw beds, and a few put their heads out over their doors. They blinked at her in surprise and nickered gently. They weren't used to being disturbed so early. "Go back to sleep," Amy whispered, kissing velvety noses as she slipped from one stall to the next.

Then she spent the next hour and a half filling water buckets, mixing feeds, and grooming. As she body-brushed each of the horses with long, firm strokes, she told them where she was going, promising that she wouldn't be gone long.

As daylight flooded over the farm, its brightness reflecting off the white boards of the farmhouse, Ty and Ben arrived.

"Don't you have a plane to catch? Why are you out here?" Ben asked, shaking his head.

"Oh, you know, just saying good-bye to the horses and telling them to behave themselves while I'm away." Amy smiled.

"OK, and what's left for us to do?" Ty asked, lifting one eyebrow and looking at her quizzically.

"You just need to turn them out," Amy admitted, holding up her hands and laughing. "I have to go in and get ready in a moment. I just want to say one last good-bye." She fished an alfalfa cube from her pocket.

Sundance whinnied as Amy approached, tossing his head up and down, making his dark mane bounce. "How is it that you always know when there's a treat in your future?" Amy said, laughing, as Sundance pushed at her hands. "There you go, greedy!"

Sundance crunched happily on the alfalfa cube while Amy rubbed him gently between the eyes. Her heart swelled with affection for the pony that her mom had bought for her. "Be a good boy," she told him. "Don't boss the others around too much, stay out of trouble, and try not to be too hard on Ty and Ben."

Sundance snorted, sounding exactly as if he were laughing at Amy's request.

She kissed him before hurrying away, reminding herself that it wouldn't be long before she would be back. She hadn't realized just how difficult leaving would be.

"Amy!" cried Lou in exasperation as Amy hurried into the farmhouse. "We're going in ten minutes, and just look at you!"

Amy looked down guiltily at her stained clothes and her dirty hands. "I'll be ready," she promised. "I just need to shower and change. My bags are already at the bottom of the stairs."

Lou reached over and plucked a piece of straw from Amy's hair. "The flight is seventeen hours. You'd better not smell like the barn if you're sitting next to me. I bet you haven't even had breakfast."

"I can grab something at the airport," Amy called over her shoulder, and headed for the stairs.

Amy had pulled on a clean white T-shirt and was looping a sweater around her waist when she heard Scott's truck pull into the yard. Scott had picked up Marnie from the bus station. Looking out the window Amy saw a slim blond girl get out of the passenger side.

Pushing her feet into a pair of sneakers, Amy pulled a comb through her long hair and tied it back into a pony-tail. She glanced at her reflection in the mirror. Her cheeks were flushed, and her gray eyes sparkled back at her. Grabbing her jacket from the chair, she ran down the stairs two at a time and arrived in the yard just as

Scott was loading the last of the bags into the truck. "All set?" he asked. "Got your passport?"

Amy double-checked her back pocket and nodded before turning to greet Marnie.

"Hi, Amy!" Marnie exclaimed. "It's great to be back at Heartland. Although I'll miss seeing you and Lou, of course."

"Thanks so much for coming to help out," said Amy, giving her a hug.

Marnie hugged her back. "No problem. You have a good time, you understand? And no worrying about what's going on here. We're going to look after everything."

Amy turned to Grandpa, who was holding the door of the truck open for her. "Good-bye, Grandpa," she said.

"Bye, honey. You call us as soon as you reach Tim and Helena's, OK?" he said before wrapping her in a huge bear hug. "I don't care if it's the middle of the night Virginia time, I want that call just the same."

"We will, first thing," she promised, hugging him fiercely before standing back so Lou could do the same.

Ben, who was driving them to the airport, climbed into the driver's seat and started the engine. Amy went to Ty, who was standing quietly nearby.

"Take care," he said, and aware of everybody's eyes on them, he hugged her briefly. "E-mail, OK?" he whispered.

Amy nodded and laughed. "Soraya's told me she expects at least three e-mails a day," she said. "What with writing to all of you, I probably won't have time to see *Dad*, never mind any of his horses!"

Ben beeped the horn, and Amy saw that Lou and Scott were already in the truck, Lou in the back, Scott in the front next to Ben.

"Take care," Amy said quietly, looking up into Ty's green eyes. Then, before she could give in to the tears that were prickling the backs of her eyes, she ran across to the truck and climbed in alongside her sister. Lou stopped chatting excitedly with Scott and gave Amy a wide grin.

Ben let out the clutch and the truck picked up speed as it moved down the long drive that led away from the farmhouse, past the paddocks on either side. Lou and Amy turned back and waved furiously until the three figures were out of sight.

"I can't believe that we're finally on our way!" Lou said. She reached over and squeezed Amy's hand, and then leaned forward to plant a kiss on Scott's cheek.

Amy felt a sharp pang at leaving Heartland, but then she began to feel the same butterflies in her stomach that she always had before a competition. "Australia," she said out loud, "here we come!"

Chapter Three

❧

"I wonder what Dad's place will look like," said Lou excitedly as the plane landed.

Amy pictured beautiful athletic horses being ridden over sprawling cross-country courses and neat stables nestled against a backdrop of trees. "I imagine it will be very professional," she mused.

"Amy!" Lou laughed. "I was thinking of Dad and Helena's house, not the stables!"

Amy caught her sister's eye and gave her a smile in return. As usual, all her thoughts had been on the horses.

The journey to Sydney, Australia, had involved two plane changes and lots of sitting around and waiting. Amy had spent the time in airports chatting with Lou and Scott and flipping through some textbooks, but she couldn't bring herself to do homework when they had just left. While she was actually in the air, she had kept herself entertained watching a couple of in-flight movies. Having hardly closed her eyes the night before, she found it easy to catch up on missed sleep, too.

Nevertheless, it had been a very long trip, and by the time the plane landed, Amy was almost bursting with the need to get to her father's ranch, which she knew was several hours' drive from Sydney.

When they finally got their bags and passed through customs, Amy hurried in front of Lou and Scott, who were strolling along happily hand in hand, and searched the crowd of people for her father.

She spotted him almost at once. His eyes were searching the crowd, and when he saw Amy, a delighted expression broke across his tanned face.

"Dad!" Amy called. Hurrying over to her father, her heart skipped with excitement. She meant to hug him, but when she reached him she suddenly felt a little awkward. She had forgotten how tall he was. Tim didn't seem to notice, though, and he caught her up in an enthusiastic embrace.

"Amy," she heard him murmur against her hair before he released her to greet Lou and Scott. Amy smiled at the sight of her sister hugging him. She noticed how Lou's fair coloring, inherited from their mother, contrasted with their father's dark curly hair. Amy couldn't help picturing how Marion and Tim must have looked as a couple.

Tim bent down to pick up two dark blue suitcases. "Both of my girls here, I can't believe it!" he said, giving them a wink.

Lou and Amy looked at each other and smiled. Amy's heart skipped. They were all together again, even if it was just for a short while.

❧

As they drove away from the airport in his Land Cruiser, Tim began discussing the details of their visit.

"Helena wanted me to let you know that she would have come to meet you, but she was anxious to make sure everything was ready for your stay," Tim told them in his strong English accent. "She was baking a chocolate cake big enough to feed us all for a week when I left." He changed gears and accelerated onto the highway. "My team at the ranch are looking forward to meeting you both."

"How many people do you have helping out on the ranch, Dad?" Lou asked.

"Sam's my manager and my right-hand man. I couldn't run the place without him," Tim explained. "Then there's Pat who does all the errands for us, trailering horses when Sam or I can't, seeing to the deliveries, and maintaining the grounds. Last, but by no means least, I have a team of eight stable hands who train the young horses we buy. They look after three horses each."

"So you have twenty-four horses at a time?" Amy commented, impressed by the number.

"Twenty-six just now," Tim corrected her. "There are currently two that I look after myself. I really want you to meet them, Amy."

"Why those two especially?" she asked.

"Ah, all will be revealed," he replied.

"Is Lily saying her first words yet, Daddy?" Lou asked with interest.

"She's making a lot of noise from dawn till dusk, but she seems to be speaking her own language most of the time." Her father chuckled. "She reminds me a lot of how you were at that age. She's crawling now and uses me as a ladder every chance she gets."

Amy watched her sister's expression soften.

"Mom said that I never left you alone," Lou remarked.

"Neither does Lily," Tim replied. "Not that I'm complaining."

Amy sat quietly, trying to make sense of the unsettled feeling that was creeping over her. It was difficult listening to her father reminisce about his time with Lou, and now with Lily, when she had spent most of her childhood apart from him.

Tim turned to Scott, who sat alongside him in the

front of the car, and changed the subject. They began to discuss Scott's schedule. He'd be staying just one evening with them before traveling to his conference, which was a three-hour drive away. He was staying there for five days of back-to-back seminars before returning to pick up Lou for their vacation. "I hear that you're going to be listening to various lectures on noninvasive therapies, but I'm curious as to which aspect most interests you," Tim asked.

Scott, who had long been interested in alternative remedies, especially when used in conjunction with conventional methods, was pleased to talk business. "I'm open to just about everything. Laser treatment, MRI, magnetic and ultrasound therapy, it all fascinates me."

While Scott spoke, Amy couldn't help but notice the pride in Lou's eyes as she listened. Amy felt a rush of pleasure for her sister. She thought how wonderful it was that Lou was able to share this with Scott, which then prompted her to think of Ty. *I wonder what he's doing now*, she thought. She knew that Virginia was fifteen hours behind in time, and it was now eight o'clock in the morning in Australia.

"Almost there," Tim suddenly announced. They had been driving for quite some time along a stretch of road with huge wheat fields on either side as far as the eye could see. He signaled right and turned the Land Cruiser onto a smaller road. Amy felt her stomach surge with excitement as they rounded a corner and a long, low building came into sight. It was a white, boarded house with a veranda running along the length of it.

"Dad, it's lovely!" Lou exclaimed.

Amy wound down her window and leaned out, her long brown hair whipping behind in the breeze. A little way from the ranch stood a pristine stable block. The closer they got to the ranch, the more it looked like something out of a horse magazine. Unlike Heartland, which was modest and compact, her father's yard obviously operated on a much larger scale. Amy could see figures moving around and two large horses in cross-ties at the end of the stable aisles.

They began driving slowly past white-railed paddocks where horses grazed on lush grass. Amy ran an experienced eye over the animals and was surprised at the differences between some of them. Most of the horses were muscled and lean, with a healthy shine to their coats. There were a few, however, that were clearly not one hundred percent fit.

"We have a few new arrivals," Tim explained, as if he knew what she was thinking. "They'll spend the next twelve months being backed and given basic training. We buy them as raw, unpolished youngsters. By the time they leave, they're fit, disciplined, and displaying top potential."

Amy recognized the mixture of pride and satisfaction in her father's voice. It was exactly how she sounded whenever she talked about the work they did at Heartland.

"What kind of time frame do you use?" Amy asked. She was interested because at Heartland they never put any time limit on a horse's rehabilitation. There was no pressure. Each horse was treated as an individual, which didn't include keeping to a schedule.

"We give them a week to settle in, just being handled and turned out each day. Then, in the next few weeks, we lunge and long-rein. The next stage is to introduce them to a bridle and saddle before backing them," her father told her. "Then they go to school and get down to the real guts of the training. Flat work, followed by jumping, and in the final stages of their time here, some experience on the show circuit. It not only increases their confidence and gives them a starting history for buyers, it also gets them known to the type of people who will be interested in buying."

"It seems very comprehensive," Lou said, sounding impressed. "I'd love to see the way you have the books organized while I'm here, if that's OK, Dad."

"Sure," Tim responded, pleased.

Amy wasn't really interested in the financial side of her father's business, but she was eager to meet the horses. "What are the names of the horses you have at the moment, Dad?" she asked quickly, before Lou could start talking finance and statistics.

"Well, if you don't mind waiting a little while longer, I'll introduce you to each one personally," Tim said, smiling. Amy nodded with a smile as her gaze met her father's in the rearview mirror.

❧

With a crunch on the gravel driveway, the Land Cruiser drew to a halt. Scott, who had fallen asleep during the trip, blinked his eyes and stretched.

As she climbed out of the car, Amy noticed a woman standing on the veranda, holding a baby in her arms. It had to be Helena. As Amy looked across at the attractive brunette she couldn't help feeling a sense of relief that Helena looked nothing like her own mom.

Helena's face broke into a smile as she made her way down the steps and walked over to greet them. "It's so lovely to meet you at last," she said warmly. "Tim has been longing to get you over here."

Tim stepped forward and formally introduced them all before scooping a gangly toddler out of Helena's arms. "This is Lily," he said proudly, looking down at the baby who was chuckling and pulling his hair. "Lily, these are your big sisters, Lou and Amy. And this is Scott. Say hello."

"Aloo," Lily managed, grinning widely.

"She's adorable," Lou enthused.

"Come on, Lily." Helena took Lily out of Tim's arms. "We'll unload the bags while you have a cuddle with your big sisters."

Before Amy knew what was happening, Helena had passed Lily to her. She took the little girl in her arms and gazed into her large brown eyes. "Hello," Amy murmured awkwardly, not knowing what else to say.

To Amy's discomfort, Lily started to look anxious. Amy tried to cradle her, but Lily started to fidget and struggle. All the while, she continued to stare at Amy, but her lips turned down at the corners and her eyes filled with tears.

Oh, no, Amy thought, *please don't cry.* But Lily began to sob, and even though Amy jiggled her, she didn't stop. If anything, her cries grew louder.

"Here," said Lou, gently lifting Lily out of Amy's arms. She held the toddler upright so she could look over her shoulder and gently hushed her, rubbing her hand gently against the toddler's small back. Within moments, Lily's cries had subsided.

"You're a natural," Helena congratulated Lou as she returned with luggage in both hands.

Everyone laughed, but Amy felt her cheeks flush. She was relieved that Lou had taken over and stopped Lily's crying, but she still felt awful that Lily had cried when she held her. And though she tried to push it away, she felt a little resentful toward Helena for thrusting Lily on her like that.

Almost as if she had guessed Amy's thoughts, Helena turned to her and smiled brightly. "Don't worry about Lily. She's in a shy stage. How was the flight?" she asked but, before Amy could answer, she continued, "You must be tired. I've got your bedroom ready. It's next to Lou's. All of our guest bedrooms are in the loft. We had it converted last year. I've laid out some clean towels for you, and there's shower gel in your bathroom. Do you want to go up now or would you rather eat first? I wasn't sure what you like, so I —"

"I think what Amy would really like is to go and see the horses," Tim interrupted with a smile.

Amy couldn't help noticing Helena's nervous chatter, and she wondered why her stepmother was trying so hard.

"Of course," Helena agreed with a quick half smile. "I should have guessed — like father, like daughter." She gave a laugh before turning to Lou and Scott. "Would you like something to eat or drink?" she asked. "I've got drinks waiting on the veranda, some snacks."

"A cold drink sounds great," Scott replied cheerfully, rolling up the sleeves of his blue shirt and stooping to pick up some of the suitcases.

Tim had obviously noticed the longing look Amy had

cast at the stable block because he turned to Scott. "Leave the bags, I'll bring them in later," he said. "You should go into the house with Helena and Lou. You must be exhausted after all those hours in the air. I'll just give Amy a quick tour of the yard."

Amy eagerly turned toward the stables before suddenly stopping and clasping her hand to her head. "I promised to call and let Grandpa know we'd arrived safely," she said.

"I'll do that," Lou offered.

"Thanks, Lou. Would you give him my love and ask him to tell Ty that I'll call him soon?"

"Sure," Lou replied, and Amy turned and followed Tim across the gravel drive to the modern stable block.

"How's Ty getting on now that he's home from the hospital?" Tim asked.

"He's doing well, but he's still not one hundred percent," Amy told him. "I just hope he doesn't push himself too hard while I'm away."

"No doubt you made it very clear to him exactly what he should and shouldn't do!" Tim said, sounding amused.

Amy bit her lip but couldn't help grinning. "Just a little," she admitted. "And I know the doctor weighed in on that subject, too, so Ty has more than enough advice to go on." As they drew closer to the yard, Amy looked from side to side, eager to see every detail.

"Most of the horses are either out being worked or in the paddocks," her father explained. "One of my stable hands, Alex, is traveling back from a three-day event with Pat and two of the horses that are just about ready to be sold."

Amy nodded. Her father's yard seemed to be every bit the well-run, professional establishment she'd been expecting.

As they crossed the yard, Tim strode ahead to run his hands over the shining palomino coat of a large gelding that was being groomed. "This is Finn. He's been with us for about six months now, so he's about halfway through his training," he told Amy. "Caroline's looking after him."

The pretty auburn-haired stable girl paused in her grooming to grin at Amy, who warmed to her instantly. "You can call me Caro; Caroline's too much of a mouthful around a stable," she said in a broad Australian accent.

"Okay, Caro," Amy said with a smile. "I bet Finn's great to ride," she went on, patting the horse's shoulder.

"You bet he is!" Caro enthused. "He's got three fantastic paces, and his dressage work is a dream."

Amy smiled at Caro, knowing immediately that they would get along well during her stay. She was just about to ask more questions about Finn when a clatter of hooves sounded behind her. Amy turned to see a girl of about her own age leading a bay horse that appeared to be at least seventeen hands high.

"That's Caspian. He's a Danish warmblood imported from Holland. He's been with us a month, and he's making Emma earn every penny of her salary!" Tim declared.

"I thought you brought your horses in from England and the States?" Amy queried.

"That's how the business started," Tim agreed, "but we've begun importing from various European countries as well."

Amy only half heard her father. Her attention was drawn to Caspian, who had suddenly stopped and was refusing to be led any farther. His nose was raised above his eyes, and Amy could see that his coat was beginning to shine with a slight sweat.

"Caspian, walk on!" Emma's voice rang sharply across the yard. She shot a rueful glance toward her observers as she tried to calm Caspian. Her ponytail was coming undone, and she looked flushed and anxious.

The more Caspian danced about, the more likely he was to step on Emma's feet, Amy thought. She watched as Emma stood at Caspian's shoulder, attempting to soothe him and walk him on at the same time. Amy frowned as she assessed the situation; it was unusual for a horse to act this way just to be difficult. She noticed that Caspian's ears were pricked forward and his nostrils were flaring widely. Following the animal's gaze, Amy saw that the last stable in the block had its door open. Sticking halfway out of the door was a wheelbarrow and fork. Somehow, an empty sack of feed was caught on the prongs of the fork, flapping gently in the breeze. Amy guessed that the noise and motion were extremely unsettling to a young, excitable horse like Caspian.

Instinctively, Amy walked across to Caspian and Emma. "Hi," she said to Emma. "I think I know what's worrying him. Do you mind if I give it a try?"

Emma hesitated for a moment and then handed Amy the lead rope. "Be careful, though. If you stand in front of him like that, you might get trampled," she pointed out. "He's bolted before."

Amy had to admit that it was nerve-racking standing in front of such a large, agitated animal instead of safely at his shoulder, but she knew that if she took on the role of a lead horse, Caspian might just calm down enough to follow her.

Presenting her back to Caspian, Amy began to walk ahead of him, applying a firm but gentle pressure to the lead rope. "C'mon, boy," she encouraged without turning around. Caspian snorted loudly, but Amy ignored him and kept going, talking soothingly and pulling the rein gently. She felt it slacken, and she knew Caspian was following her. As they drew level with the open stable door, Caspian blew air heavily out of his nostrils and skittered sideways, but Amy continued walking forward until they were past. Then she turned to the horse and gently stroked his neck. In return, Caspian stood quietly, even though Amy could still feel the tension in his muscles. Emma had followed them, and without a word she now took the rope back from Amy.

"I think he was just scared. From a distance, that feed sack must have looked pretty fierce," Amy said with a short laugh.

"Thanks," Emma replied, not looking at Amy but concentrating instead on stroking Caspian's neck. Tim and Caro joined them.

"Wow, Caspian's a hard nut to crack. How did you get him to follow you like that?" Tim asked.

Caro raised her eyebrows. "Yeah, what's your secret?"

Amy smiled, appreciating their interest. "When a horse is scared he often just needs a bit of reassurance. In the wild he would follow the alpha horse past a scary object, so I just took the lead and hoped his natural instincts would take over and make him follow me," she explained.

"Well, it worked," her father said happily.

"It did," Emma agreed. "Thanks." She clicked with her tongue and led the bay gelding away.

Amy watched them go and couldn't help feeling that somehow she had done the wrong thing. But before she had time to try to figure out why, Tim steered her away from Caro and into the tack room at the end of the stable block.

Unlike Heartland's tack room, which was always cluttered, Tim's tack room was large and airy, with saddles lining three walls and bridles hanging neatly on hooks underneath. The room had the familiar smell of saddle soap, and Amy noticed that well-stocked grooming kits filled tidy cubby holes at the back.

"This is great!" she exclaimed, turning her attention to the one wall that didn't have tack on it. Row upon row of blue, red, and yellow ribbons lined it, alongside shelves of silver cups and plaques. But what really drew Amy's gaze was the pictures.

"Pegasus!" she whispered, walking up to take a closer look. It was on Pegasus that Tim had suffered the accident that had ended his show-jumping days. After Tim left, Amy's mom had taken Pegasus to her father's farm in Virginia and nursed him back to full health using alternative remedies.

One particular picture made Amy's stomach churn with emotion. It showed Tim and Marion standing on either side of Pegasus, who had his ears pricked forward attentively. On his back was a young girl who Amy immediately recognized as Lou. They all looked so happy that it made the back of Amy's throat ache, and her eyes began to sting with tears. Pegasus was a part of the family history — part of the best and the hardest memories.

She turned to her father, and he gave her a knowing smile in return.

"Come on," said Tim softly. "We have two other residents that I want to introduce you to now."

Amy was very curious about the horses she was going to meet. Tim led her around the side of the stable block to the second row of box stalls. He pulled back the bolt on the first door and Amy stepped inside. She gasped with pleasure at the beautiful horse that stood looking at her. "What's his name?" she asked, without taking her eyes off the flea-bitten gray gelding. His long silver mane and tail gave him striking looks.

"Spirit," Tim answered. "And he's yours for the time that you're here," he added.

"Really?" Amy couldn't disguise her delight as she ran her eyes over his sloping shoulder and took in the kind expression in his large, dark eyes. Amy knew instinctively that he was a very special horse.

"Of course, I do have a slight hidden agenda," her father admitted.

"How slight?" Amy demanded, pretending to be stern.

"I was hoping you would put in some work on him," Tim replied seriously. "I bought him just over a year ago. Helena fell in love with him, so I decided to let her take on training him."

"I didn't realize that Helena was so interested in horses," Amy said in surprise.

Tim nodded. "It's how I met her. She'd been staying with a friend in England. The day before her friend was going to ride in a competition, she broke a bone in her wrist. Helena had always ridden, so she took her friend's place. She came in third in the dressage class, one place below the sire of a youngster I was thinking of buying. I had wanted to see the sire perform before I agreed to purchase the yearling — but I ended up asking Helena out to dinner." He gave a small laugh and ran his hand through his curly hair.

"Anyway, we've had no problem with Spirit until recently," Tim went on. "He developed into an amazing event horse, and we could all see that he had the potential to make it to the very top. But Helena eased up on her training to spend more time with Lily. When I sent Spirit out to shows with different riders, his performance just wasn't anywhere near what we had come to expect. It was as if he had lost all enthusiasm for what he was doing. It didn't take me long to work out that he only shines when Helena is riding him. They have this amazing bond between them that, unfortunately, we have to break if we're going to be able to sell him. Helena has stopped riding Spirit over the past couple of weeks, and I was hoping that you would spend some time with him every day that you're here." He turned to face Amy and winked. "That is, unless you've come here to have a break from riding?"

"A vacation without riding? Never!" Amy laughed and walked over to Spirit who had been watching them with interest. She bent down to blow into his nostrils, greeting the horse as another horse would. He blew back heavily, accepting her at once.

"He's lovely, Dad," she said happily.

"That's that then. I know you're going to love riding him. He has fantastic elevated paces," her father told her, leading the way out of the box. "Now, let me introduce you to my second project."

A coal-black head was looking over the door of the adjoining box. "This," Tim told Amy, "is Mistral."

Amy didn't think she had ever seen such a stunning horse. "She's an Andalusian, right?" she asked, thinking of the famous Spanish horses. She'd never seen a black one before.

"She's part Andalusian. Actually, she's a Thoroughbred cross," Tim answered as Mistral snaked her head back into the stall. "The breed is becoming quite popular in Australia because they're very fast and they can turn on a dollar. In Spain they're used for bullfighting, so it's not surprising they're agile — think of the twists and turns they have to perform in a bull ring. There are studs in quite a few states over here now, and they compete in dressage, show jumping, and cross-country events."

"Where did she go?" Amy asked, surprised to see that

Mistral had retreated to the far corner of the stall. It was not a reaction she usually got from a horse.

"Well, that's the strange thing about her," Tim said, joining Amy at the door of the box. Mistral was standing as far away from them as possible. Her strong, proud neck hung low, her haunches taut. "She's something of a mystery," Tim went on. "She just doesn't seem to like human company at all. Whenever we try and work with her she breaks into a heavy sweat and gets so distressed we have to stop. I imported her six weeks ago from Spain. By now she should be starting to work on basic schooling, but we can't even lunge her without causing her stress. I'm afraid I can only give her a few more weeks before I'll have to cut my losses and sell her, which would be a real waste of potential. Do you think you can do anything with her?"

"I'll certainly try," Amy promised. Her mind automatically began to race through the methods she would try with Mistral and Spirit. She was proud that her father had so much confidence in her skills but, most of all, she couldn't wait to spend time with both horses, getting to know them and, hopefully, helping them through their difficulties. Her heart soared as she considered the weeks ahead. It looked as if staying with her father was going to be even more exciting than she had ever dreamed!

Chapter Four

Amy leaned out the window and gave a contented sigh. From her room she had views over the fields that stretched away from the ranch. Two chestnut horses in the closest field were chasing each other playfully. Amy smiled as they cantered in circles, their tails held high.

"Are you ready?" Lou asked, coming into the room. "Dad and Helena have organized a welcome party for us so we can meet everyone here."

"Sounds great," Amy said, turning around and noticing that her sister had changed into beige pants and a cotton sweater. Amy still had on her clothes from the plane.

"I've just been helping Helena put Lily to bed," Lou told her. "She's so sweet. She grabbed hold of my finger and wouldn't let go."

Amy tried not to think of Lily's initial reaction to her. She slipped a jacket on and followed Lou downstairs and out onto the back patio.

❧

Outside, the patio was crowded with people standing in small groups, illuminated by colorful Chinese lanterns strung overhead. Amy and Lou were introduced to all the people who helped in their father's business. Amy smiled and answered their questions about Heartland enthusiastically, while trying to make a mental note of everyone's name.

"This is terrific," a tall, slim boy with red hair remarked. He was looking hungrily at the bowls of chips, platters of chicken, relish, boiled eggs, and steaming corn on the cob that were spread over a long trestle table. "I usually go home to beans on toast, so thanks for putting your dad up to this feast," he added with a grin.

Amy laughed as he passed her a plate.

Caro came over to join them. "How did you do at your show, Alex?" she asked. Alex's blue eyes crinkled at the corners. "Great, thanks. We placed first — as you might expect!" he declared.

"Show-off," Caro teased, rolling her eyes toward Amy.

"Just because you only come home with yellow ribbons there's no need to take your insecurities out on me," Alex replied, shaking his head playfully.

Emma, who was standing a little way off, overheard this last comment and laughed. "At least *we* know there's more to competitions than the prizes," she retorted.

Alex pretended to look shocked. "Rubbish! It's a good thing Tim's got me to rely on."

Tim turned from the barbecue and brandished his spatula. "OK, you guys," he said, "do you think you can take a break from squabbling long enough to eat?"

"Anything you say, boss!" Alex grinned, holding out his plate.

Tim began to pile the plates with burgers and sausages. When he reached a large, balding man who was sitting a little way from the group, he paused. "Do you have an hour to drive into town with me tomorrow, Sam?" Amy heard him ask.

"Shouldn't be a problem, Tim," the stable manager replied between mouthfuls of potato salad.

Caro unfolded chairs for herself and Amy, close to the warmth of the barbecue. "Sam never says much. He only talks when he has to," she commented softly. "But he does sometimes ask Alex why he insists on talking so much when he has so little worth saying!"

Amy laughed and glanced at Alex. He was the type of person you couldn't help liking. He was talking animatedly now to a man she had not yet met. The man was in his thirties, with black, wavy hair and bright blue eyes.

"That's Pat," Caro told her, following her gaze.

Just then, Helena made her way over to them. "Did you get to meet Spirit and Mistral?" she asked as she dragged a chair over and sat down next to Amy.

Amy nodded in reply.

"What did you think of them?" Helena asked.

"They're both lovely-looking horses," Amy replied enthusiastically. "And I've never worked with a horse that is part Andalusian before. I can't wait to see Mistral move — I bet she has an amazing stride! Spirit is beautiful, too. I can tell just by looking at him that he's got a wonderful personality."

Helena nodded and smiled. "I expect Tim told you that Spirit was my horse?"

"Yes, he said that you turned him into an amazing eventer," Amy told her.

"Really?" Helena laughed and raised an eyebrow at Tim. "He's never said that to me. He usually complains that I spoiled him."

Everyone laughed as Tim and Helena exchanged rueful glances. Amy, like the others, felt the warmth between the couple. She smiled, but inside she was struggling with emotion. She couldn't remember her mom and dad

being together. Tim had met and married Helena a few
years ago. Amy knew it wasn't fair that she should find
it difficult being around Tim and his new wife, but she
still felt reserved and somewhat awkward.

As Amy wrestled with her feelings, she noticed that
Helena had turned to Scott and was asking him about
the upcoming conference. That left Amy free to wander
across the patio to ask Emma about her work with
Caspian that afternoon.

"He was fine," Emma replied shortly, then immediately turned to Alex and began a discussion about the
best way to jump a course she had set up in one of the
training rings.

Amy was discouraged by the fact that Emma didn't
want to start a conversation with her. She wondered
why, but she tried not to dwell on it — after all, everyone else had been friendly and welcoming. And it was
far more worthwhile to think ahead to her time with
Spirit and Mistral.

✺

Later that evening, Amy called Ty, hoping to reach
him at home before he left for Heartland. She felt a rush
of homesickness the moment she heard the familiar sound
of his voice.

"How's it going?" he asked warmly.

"OK," she replied, and immediately launched into a million questions. "How are you and Grandpa? Is Marnie managing OK? What about Ben and Red — and how's Dazzle coming along?"

"Hey, slow down!" Ty laughed. "We're all fine. Ben's really pleased with how Red's jumping, and Dazzle is getting better with every session. He seems to be really enjoying the work now. Your grandpa's following all Lou's instructions to the word, and Marnie's fitting in just fine."

"And the rest of the horses?" Amy asked anxiously.

"Amy!" Ty said firmly. "You've got to stop worrying about things here. You're supposed to be enjoying your time with your family. So, tell me what's happened since you got there."

Amy quickly filled him in on everyone she had met and then went on to talk about the horses — especially Spirit and Mistral.

Ty listened attentively. "They sound great. Just don't spend so much time working with the horses that you miss out on time with your dad," he reminded her.

Amy sighed. She knew it was a good point, she just found the horses so much easier to relate to. "I miss you," she said quietly.

"I miss you, too," Ty replied.

❧

Amy woke the next morning to find she had slept for a full twelve hours. She couldn't remember the last time she had slept for that long. All the traveling had obviously worn her out. She quickly pulled on some clothes and hurried downstairs just in time to say good-bye to Scott as he left for his conference.

Scott and Tim were stowing his bags in the truck, with Lou standing nearby.

"That's it," said Scott, gently laying his blazer over the luggage. His eyes suddenly lighted on Amy. "I thought you were never going to wake up! Thanks for seeing me off," he said, before turning to hug Lou good-bye.

Tim was holding the door open for him. "Thanks for everything," said Scott as he shook Tim's hand.

"No problem," Tim replied. "I'll be interested in hearing about it when you get back."

Pat started the engine and, as the truck rolled away, Amy noticed a wistful look in Lou's eyes. "He'll be back soon," she said, and squeezed her sister's arm.

"I know," Lou made an effort to look happier. "And I'm really looking forward to today. Helena and I are taking Lily into town and then we're having tea at a neighbor's ranch. Do you want to come?"

Amy thought about it for a moment, but she was longing to get down to the yard and see the horses. She shook her head. "I'd love to, but . . . ," she began.

"I know, I know." Lou laughed. "You want to get started with Spirit and Mistral."

Amy smiled. "Maybe we can go for a ride together this afternoon?" she suggested.

"I think we're going to be gone for most of the day. I'm sure we'll get a chance to ride together soon, though," Lou promised.

There was the sound of footsteps crunching on the gravel as Helena joined them. "How about a nice big breakfast to set you up for the day?" she smiled. "I've made hash browns, eggs, and bacon."

They all walked back inside. Lou and Helena talked happily about their schedule for the day, and Amy's thoughts drifted away to her own plans for Spirit and Mistral.

✀

Amy decided to work with Mistral first. When she went into the box stall with a lead rope in her hand, the big black horse snorted nervously and backed into the far corner. Amy slowly shook her head as she gazed at the mare. Her eyes were large, bright, and placed wide apart, which told Amy that Mistral had a kind temperament. It didn't make sense that she was so nervous around people. Tim had assured Amy that Mistral's only previous owner had a good reputation.

Amy chatted reassuringly to Mistral as she clipped the

rope on her halter and led her out to the training arenas behind the ranch. Emma was in the jumping ring, and Amy paused to watch her ride a showy chestnut over a course of eight jumps. They moved together in perfect symmetry, and Amy realized that Emma was a first-class rider, giving exactly the right balance of encouragement and guidance to the young horse.

Mistral began to grow a little restless, and Amy led her into the center of the all-weather arena before halting again. She knew that joining up with Mistral was the best way to gain her trust. She unclipped the lead rope, and Mistral instantly moved away from her. It was clear that the mare didn't want to share her personal space.

Amy flicked the end of the rope toward the mare's hindquarters, and Mistral swung away to the outside of the arena. Patches of sweat were already forming on her flanks. Amy flicked the rope again and Mistral began to canter around. After a while, Amy became concerned. Mistral was showing all the signs of misery. Amy would have expected the mare to have started to relax after several laps of the ring, but her tail was still clamped tightly down, her eyes were wide with tension, and her nostrils were flaring. Amy persevered, hoping that the mare would soon show signs of wanting to join her in the center of the ring. But Mistral's fatigue was obvious. Her sides were heaving, and her pace was slowing.

"She's really not that fit, you know," a young girl

spoke, breaking Amy's concentration. Amy recognized the voice as Emma's. Amy glanced across to the entrance of the arena where the girl stood watching. Mistral took advantage of Amy's lapse in concentration to halt in the far corner. Amy sighed. She knew it would be best now to cut her losses and call an end to the session. Mistral was too tired to begin all over again. As she walked over to get Mistral, Amy noticed Emma give her a slightly disapproving look before leading the chestnut away.

Amy stuck her chin out mutinously at Emma's retreating figure. "She doesn't know what I was trying to do, does she?" Amy murmured to the mare as she led her back to the yard. "The problem is," she added sadly, "neither do you."

❧

After Amy cooled Mistral, she carried Spirit's tack to his stall. The horse looked at her with interest, and Amy couldn't help breathing a sigh of relief that he seemed pleased at the prospect of being ridden.

She warmed him up and then began to practice some basic schooling patterns. Spirit obeyed her perfectly, but that's all it was, obedience — a well-trained horse carrying out her commands. Everything she did with Spirit felt flat; he simply wasn't open to partnering with her.

She spoke encouragingly and noticed that his ear barely flickered back. "Let's see how you jump," she said to him, and pointed him at a practice fence in the middle of the ring. As they approached the jump, Amy noticed that there was no surge of enthusiasm — not the excited gathering of muscles or extended stride Amy would usually expect. If Spirit had been human he would have yawned as he popped over the jump, rattling the top bar with his hooves.

⚜

Tim was waiting for her when she got back to the stables. "How did it go?" he asked as he opened the box stall door.

"Hmmm," Amy replied. "You were right about his lack of enthusiasm." She slipped off Spirit and led him into his box.

"Give it some time," Tim advised. "This was your first go."

Amy nodded. "If I make out a list, is there a health-food shop in town where you could buy some herbs and remedies for me?" she asked.

"I think so," Tim replied. "Leave it with me."

⚜

Amy helped herself to a sandwich Helena had thoughtfully left out for her lunch. Then she went back down onto the yard to see if there was anything she could do.

Emma was outside the stable block with Caspian,

picking out his hooves. Amy decided to try to make an effort. "Hi," she called. "Do you want a hand?"

"I can manage, thanks," Emma said. Before Amy could reply, Emma went on in the same expressionless tone. "I've been picking hooves for over ten years. I've got it down now."

Amy felt her cheeks burn. She had no idea what Emma was implying. Placing her hands on her hips, Amy opened her mouth to reply, but Emma ignored her. The stable hand tugged Caspian's slip tie loose and led him away.

As Amy stood staring at Emma's back she heard a movement behind her.

"Alex and I were just about to go for a ride," Caro said, and smiled. "If you'd like to come along, you could ride Jinx for me. You'd be doing me a favor — I won't have to exercise him later, and it'll be good for him to start getting used to different riders."

Amy couldn't tell if Caro had overheard her exchange with Emma, but she felt a rush of relief at her friendliness. "That sounds great," she said warmly.

∾

Within ten minutes, the trio was clattering out of the yard. Alex was riding a big black gelding named Zeus. "He already has a buyer lined up," Alex said, patting his neck. "We're just finessing gaits and timing now."

"He's in great shape," Amy remarked. Zeus didn't have a spare ounce of fat on him and was clearly at the peak of fitness.

"Why, thanks, sport. Now then, Miss Fleming, are you up to tackling our cross-country course or do you want something a little more sedate?" Alex asked in a deliberately exaggerated Australian accent.

Amy laughed and felt a small thrill at the thought of taking Jinx over a full course. It was just what she needed after her difficult morning. "Let's go for it," she said eagerly.

"The course starts just on the other side of those trees to your right," Caro said, pointing. "Jinx has a very bold jump but he can be a bit of a baby on the approach, so he needs to feel that you're with him every step of the way."

Amy nodded and patted Jinx's golden neck reassuringly before shortening her stirrups.

As they rode through an opening in the trees, Amy saw an impressive array of fences that stretched over two fields and disappeared into the distance.

"There's no jump higher than one meter, OK?" Alex said.

Amy nodded.

"If you let me get one jump in front of you, then follow the line that I take, you'll be fine," Alex assured her. "Caro will come last."

They all checked their girths and began to warm up the

horses. When Alex left them to tackle the first jump — a huge felled tree trunk — Jinx snorted and plunged. Amy calmed him by asking him to accept the bit, and, after he had collected his stride, she sent him forward. Jinx flew over the tree with a powerful surge, and Amy felt a rush of adrenaline. She had to remind herself to hold Jinx at a steady canter even though she would have liked to let him open up into a gallop. "Steady now. You may know your way around, but I don't," she murmured as a combination loomed in front of them.

The rest of the course passed by in a blur, and Jinx didn't falter once. Under Amy's guidance he cleared each jump with an exuberance that left her breathless by the time she rode up next to Alex. "That was incredible!" she exclaimed with delight.

"You both look as if you could go around again," Alex said.

"Wow. Jinx certainly has taken to you," Caro told Amy.

"He was fantastic," Amy admitted as they turned for home. They went at a slow pace to give the horses the opportunity to cool down.

"Do you have a course back home?" Alex asked.

Amy smiled, thinking of the basic facilities they had at Heartland. "Everything we have is geared toward rehabilitating the horses that come to us. We have some jumps in one of the rings, but mostly we work on the flat," she explained.

"Tim said that you do a lot of alternative stuff," Caro remarked.

"Sounds like a bit of a waste of time to me," Alex commented. "No offense," he added hurriedly as Caro frowned at him.

"It's OK. Ben, one of our stable hands, was pretty skeptical when he first joined us." Amy smiled. "He's come around now that he's seen the results."

"Your dad certainly thinks it has a lot going for it," Alex admitted. "He's definitely mentioned the work that you do."

"It's not just me," said Amy quickly. "I couldn't do it without Ty and Ben and Lou and Grandpa — we're a team."

"It's the same here," Caro said, nodding her head. "I think the main reason we get such good results with the horses is because we work so well together."

Amy became quiet as she thought about Caro's words.

"Are you OK?" Caro asked, as they rode into the yard.

Amy saw concern written across Caro's face and thought again how nice she was. "I'm just feeling a little bad that I've left everyone else to do all the work at home while I'm here," she admitted.

"I understand that. If I'm away from here, even for a

long weekend, I start itching to come back. After all, no one can look after my horses as well as I can!" Caro joked, but then a serious expression came into her eyes. "You shouldn't feel bad. What you do at Heartland is great, but you've got other important things in your life, too — like family."

Amy nodded. She knew that what Caro was saying made sense, but she had given Heartland the very best of what she had to offer ever since her mom's death. Now she found it difficult to do anything else.

❧

After showering and changing, Amy wandered down to the kitchen to find Lou playing with Lily in her high chair. Helena was busy making a pasta sauce, and Amy volunteered to set the table.

"Actually, I've already set it out on the veranda tonight. But it would be great if you could feed Lily her dinner for me — it's in the bowl on the table," Helena answered.

Amy looked at the green plastic bowl and then at Lily, who was staring at her. She picked up the bowl. "Sure, no problem," she replied, feeling rather apprehensive as she sat down next to Lily.

"How did your day go?" Lou asked, getting up and filling a pan with boiling water.

"Um, OK," said Amy distractedly as she tried to persuade Lily to eat. It was some kind of vegetable stew. Amy thought it looked disgusting — especially as clumps oozed back out of Lily's mouth.

"Here," Helena said, smiling and passing her a napkin.

Amy tried not to make a face as she wiped the slobbery goo away from Lily's mouth. Unfortunately, the more she wiped, the more of Lily's face it seemed to cover. Lily pushed at the napkin, getting the sticky glop all over her hands, too.

"How did your sessions go with the horses?" Helena asked.

"Not great, but then they rarely do in the early stages," Amy responded. For some reason she was feeling a little defensive, but neither Lou nor Helena seemed to notice.

"I always found that Spirit responded well when I told him what we were going to do before we actually went through the paces," Helena commented. "That way it felt as if we were in on it together, rather than my just asking him to obey."

Amy felt a stirring of resentment at Helena's advice. A slight frown creased her forehead. She didn't know what was wrong; normally, she appreciated other people's input. She decided her frustration must be a side effect of jet lag, and she returned her attention to Lily.

Amy tried to make Lily more interested in her meal by

talking to her. "Mmm, Lily, look, yummy food just for you," she offered. But Lily pressed her lips into a thin line and refused to eat any more.

"I'm sorry," Amy said, "she just doesn't want it."

"Here, you finish the spaghetti," Lou said, taking over. Lou pretended that the spoon of food was an airplane and zoomed it toward Lily's mouth. Lily giggled and opened wide.

As Lou and Helena chatted easily, Amy concentrated on stirring the spaghetti. *Why won't Lily respond to me?* she thought, glancing at the baby who was now smiling happily up at Lou. Amy sighed inwardly and tried not to listen to the voice in her head — the one that said maybe she just didn't belong in her dad's new family.

Chapter Five

After a couple of days at her father's ranch, Amy managed to find time to send some e-mails home. She leaned back in her chair and read over the last few lines of her message to Soraya. *I think that Spirit might end up being as difficult to reach as Mistral. I hope that I can make a difference before I have to head back.*

Just as she was about to add another line, she heard her sister's bedroom door open. Amy left the computer and looked out into the hallway.

"Morning," Lou said.

"Hi," Amy replied. "I'm just finishing an e-mail and then, after breakfast, I'm going to work with Spirit and Mistral. Do you want to come down and meet them?"

"I'd love to," Lou agreed eagerly. Then she clapped

her hand to her head. "Oh, I forgot! I'm really sorry, I've already arranged to go out hiking with Helena this morning. We're going to put Lily in her baby carrier and hike up to one of the local scenic views. Why don't you come with us?"

"I would," said Amy regretfully, "but I've planned to concentrate on Spirit and Mistral this morning. I really need to join up with Mistral. We didn't have a very successful session yesterday."

Lou looked sympathetic. "Can't it wait for this afternoon? We won't be out long."

"I feel better doing it first thing. The yard gets busy later in the day. I'll put aside some time for Lily soon," Amy promised.

"I hope so. I was beginning to think she needed to grow a mane and tail to get your attention." Lou sighed.

Amy felt a little guilty. Then she caught sight of the mischievous twinkle in her sister's eyes and they both burst into laughter.

❧

"You could have made a bit more of an effort," Amy muttered as she led Spirit back into his stall. Once again he had behaved impeccably, but his performance lacked spark. He had no conviction. He had tipped the poles on most of the jumps, and his flatwork was just that, flat.

"You've got to try harder," she told him sternly. Amy knew trainers had techniques for horses like Spirit, horses that were just going through the paces. Some trainers would rap horses' legs as they cleared a fence, frightening them into jumping cleaner, tighter. But Amy didn't endorse that practice, and she was certain Spirit was a special case. He had athletic ability to spare. It was an emotional investment that he lacked.

Spirit rubbed his head against her arm where he was itching under his bridle, drawing Amy from her contemplation.

"OK, OK," she sighed. "I get the message."

❧

When Amy let herself into Mistral's box, the mare regarded her suspiciously but, for the first time, didn't back away from her. Amy had spent ages grooming her before breakfast, and Mistral's coal-black coat gleamed. The mare had appeared to relax toward the end of the grooming session, and Amy wanted to try to recapture that mood before taking her to the ring. She tipped a little lavender oil into her hands and began to massage it into Mistral's coat, hoping the oil's relaxing qualities would help.

After five minutes, Amy slipped Mistral's halter on. Immediately, the mare grew tense. "Easy," Amy said to soothe her, and returned to massaging Mistral's neck, in small T-touch circles, until she felt the muscles relax again. "OK, girl, walk on," Amy said, and led her from the box.

♌

Once in the middle of the training ring, Amy released Mistral and tapped her lightly on the hindquarters to send her to the edge of the ring. The black horse broke into a powerful trot, and Amy took up an aggressive stance to encourage her into a canter. Mistral completed five circuits before Amy sent her around in the opposite direction. It took a while, but eventually Mistral began to show signs of wanting to join Amy in the center of the ring. Amy turned her body sideways and lowered her eyes. She needed Mistral to sense that she was not a threat to her. She could hear Mistral slow her pace until she came to a halt. Then came the sound that Amy was waiting for, the soft, padded thud of hooves on sand as Mistral made her way to Amy.

"Good girl," Amy whispered as she moved away and Mistral followed. Amy wanted to make a fuss over her but knew that Mistral would flinch away from the attention, so Amy quietly clipped the lead rein back onto the mare's halter and started back to the yard. As she left the arena, she noticed Emma watching her. Amy didn't know how long she had been there but, when she raised her hand in a friendly wave, Emma quickly turned away.

Amy sighed. She was beginning to think Emma was even more of an enigma than Mistral or Spirit.

❧

After turning Spirit and Mistral out in the paddocks, Amy wandered back to the ranch house. Lou was pushing Lily gently on a tire swing that Tim had made for her. He had fashioned a head, tail, and saddle for the tire to make a swaying horse, and Lily was gurgling with laughter at every push.

Lou saw Amy and paused. "How were the horses?" she asked.

Before Amy could tell her sister about her progress with Mistral, Lily called out, "More. Oooh, more."

"Oooh?" Amy asked, raising an eyebrow.

"It's what she calls me," Lou said shyly. "She started saying it this morning."

The screen door banged, and Helena appeared on the veranda, carrying bowls of salad. "Hi," she said, and smiled. "Tim's just washing up inside. We'll have lunch as soon as he's ready."

"I'd better clean up, too," said Amy. "I won't be long."

When she came back, Tim was sitting at the table, drinking a glass of water. It was the first time he had joined them for lunch. Amy hadn't realized just how busy he would be. She thought of how hard she worked at Heartland and knew it must be the same for her father here. But she was determined to make more of an effort to spend time with him.

"Hi," Tim said, looking up. "How did it go today?"

"Good, thanks," replied Amy enthusiastically. She told him about joining up with Mistral.

Tim listened intently. "Well done," he said warmly when Amy had finished.

"It's only the first small step," Amy added quickly.

"But at least it's in the right direction," Helena put in. She glanced up at Amy and Tim. "How do the two of you feel about going for a ride this afternoon? Lou offered to babysit Lily, so I thought we could ride down to Fiddler's Creek."

"That sounds like a great idea. I have a little free time this afternoon," Tim agreed enthusiastically. He turned to Lou. "Are you sure you don't mind? You haven't ridden at all yet."

"It's fine," Lou assured him. "I'm going to do some finger painting with Lily."

Amy glanced at her sister and was struck by how happy and relaxed she looked. Her blue eyes shone brightly, and already her skin had a slight glow from the warm Australian sun. Amy was pleased Lou had offered to watch Lily, but she also wanted her to go on a ride with their father. "Thanks, Lou," she said warmly. "Then maybe you can go for a ride tomorrow?"

"No worries. I'm sure I'll get plenty of chances for

that," Lou replied. She lifted Lily out of her high chair. "Let's go find your smock," she said, breaking into a wide smile as Lily reached up to her.

Amy suddenly remembered that she had promised Lou she would spend some time getting to know Lily better. *I'll do something with her tomorrow,* she thought.

✍

Amy was tightening Spirit's girth when Tim and Helena led their horses around from the other side of the stable block. Spirit stiffened when he caught sight of Helena. He let out a long nicker and strained his neck to reach her.

Amy glanced up to see a frustrated look on Helena's face as she smoothed Spirit's nose and turned away. It was clear that she would have loved to give Spirit more attention. Amy suddenly felt a stab of sympathy for Helena. She knew how fulfilling it was to share a deep bond with a horse — and how difficult it must be for Helena to have to keep her distance.

"She's a beauty," Amy said to Helena, trying to lighten the mood.

"Isn't she?" Helena smiled, stroking the satiny neck of the small horse she was riding. "Her name's Lace. She's pure Arabian."

"Ready?" Tim interrupted as the large gelding he was riding began to fidget and stamp his hooves. Amy swung herself lightly into the saddle and shortened her reins. "All set," she told him.

❧

It took just under an hour to reach the creek. As the horses lowered their heads to drink from the water, Helena complimented Amy on her riding. "Spirit goes very well for you," she said.

"Maybe now, but not in the ring," Amy replied with a grimace, making Helena and Tim laugh.

"I have a feeling you're going to have a breakthrough with him. Just keep trying," said Helena, encouraging her with a smile.

"Thanks," Amy said and, looking into Helena's sincere brown eyes, she felt, for the first time, a slight warming toward her.

They made their way along the winding, tree-lined track, back toward the ranch, and Amy thought about how nice it would be if she could get along with Helena in the same way that Lou did. *Why is it so easy for Lou?* Amy asked herself as she leaned forward and flipped Spirit's mane so that it was all lying on the same side of his neck. She thought about how effortlessly open and candid Lou was with Helena. But, as Amy followed her father's wife on the trail, she knew that she just didn't feel the same way.

🞡

After they had ridden back to the ranch and seen to the horses, Helena suggested they have cold drinks on the veranda. As they approached the house, Amy saw Lou and Lily waving to them.

Tim's face broke into a big smile as he held out his arms to Lily. "How's my beautiful girl?" he asked, lifting her up onto his shoulders.

Lily squealed with laughter and held out her hands to Helena.

Helena rescued her and stood her on the ground. "Why don't you sit on Amy's lap while Mummy gets some drinks?" she suggested.

Amy remembered her promise to spend more time with Lily. She walked across and smiled down at the little girl. "Do you want me to push you on your horse swing, Lily?" she asked gently.

Lily stared at Amy solemnly for a moment before raising her arms, signaling she wanted to be picked up. Delighted, Amy lifted her onto the tire swing and began to push. Lily giggled happily as she swung back and forth, and Amy felt a rush of relief and surprise that Lily was having such a good time. And, Amy had to admit, so was she.

After a few minutes, the screen door banged and Lou

emerged with a tray of glasses. "Oooh, Oooh," Lily called the moment she saw her. She began to wriggle in the swing seat. Amy hurriedly brought the tire to a stop and lifted Lily up. But before she had a chance to do anything, Lily squirmed in her arms. "Oooh!" she called again.

Lou rushed over from the patio and took Lily. "It's just because I've spent a lot of time with her, that's all," she said, obviously trying to make Amy feel better.

Amy bit her lip and gave Lou a nod, but inside she was disappointed. She had just begun to imagine herself as Lily's sister, as part of the family, and now she felt like an outsider once again.

🙊

After Lily had been put to bed that evening, Tim showed Amy the den and produced a home video from his library. "This will give you a good idea of Spirit's potential," he explained. "I filmed Helena riding a preliminary test. Watch it and see what you think." He clicked the VCR on and snapped off the light so that the room was in darkness. Amy leaned forward to concentrate on the screen.

Although the test was a novice one, from the moment Spirit entered the arena to the moment he departed, there was no doubting his potential for greatness. Amy searched for the right word to describe him, and the one that came to mind was *sparkle.* He performed every action with a zest that left other horses looking dull and lifeless by comparison.

She watched the video three times, noting the way Helena and Spirit seemed to know what the other was thinking. The bond between them was obvious.

"Well?" asked Tim when Amy switched off the television. "Do you think you can get him back on track?"

"I don't know," Amy admitted honestly. "His performance on the tape is awesome, but I'm not sure where that horse went." She looked thoughtful. "If we're going to get him back, I think the first stage is for him to bond with me — but not too much, or we might be faced with the same problem again." She smiled ruefully. "The next step will be to have other people ride him, too. That way, he won't have the option of bonding too strongly with just one person." As she spoke she was filled with a new optimism. She now felt certain she could overcome Spirit's problems, and she couldn't wait to start working with him again.

🙡

Amy spent an hour with Mistral the following morning before breakfast, grooming and talking to her. As soon as the mare relaxed she led her down to the schooling ring.

Amy noticed her father and Emma standing ringside, poised to watch. As she snapped the lunging line onto the mare's halter, she silently willed Mistral to cooperate, but Mistral fidgeted nervously.

"It's OK," Amy said before sending the horse away.

She clicked to Mistral to walk around the ring, but the mare refused to move. The whites of her eyes were flashing, and her ears went flat against her head. Amy flicked her whip slightly to encourage Mistral forward but, instead, the mare skidded backward and reared in the air. Amy pulled the lead line taut, terrified that Mistral might fall over and hurt herself.

As soon as the mare dropped back down to the ground Amy walked over to her, speaking in low, comforting tones the whole time. A lather of sweat and sand covered Mistral's coat. "It's OK, it's OK," Amy said as she deftly unbuckled the halter.

As soon as she was free, Mistral snorted and recklessly wheeled away. Amy thought fast. She didn't want to distress the mare more, yet she couldn't leave the training session on such an unsuccessful note. If she did, she knew that the setback would impede the progress of future sessions.

Amy knew she had to take control of the situation. She returned to her position in the center of the ring and, using the schooling whip, made Mistral stay out on the track and complete circuits in a controlled trot. She asked the horse to change direction twice, all the time reinforcing the fact that she was in charge.

After five minutes, Amy was satisfied that she had salvaged the training session, and she allowed Mistral to halt.

"Nice work," Tim said, holding the gate open for her.

Amy had been so engrossed with Mistral that she had forgotten all about Tim and Emma watching.

"I didn't think you'd get her to cooperate after the lunging, but you did exactly the right thing," he continued, running his eyes over the mare.

"She's a challenge. You can't take anything for granted with her," Amy said, her strained voice hinting at frustration. "You're sure she wasn't mistreated?"

Tim shook his head. "It did cross my mind," he admitted. "But she was sold to me as unbacked and from a reputable yard. I know that there are places that break their horses using harsh methods, but that wouldn't apply in this case."

Emma followed a couple of steps behind as they walked back up to the yard.

"I asked Emma to come with me because I have a suggestion for you both," Tim began. He glanced at Amy. "How are you managing your load, handling both Spirit and Mistral?" Amy wasn't sure what this had to do with her and Emma, but she smiled as she replied, "Fine, Dad, I'm used to doing a lot more back home. I'd love it if there was something else I could do around the yard."

"That's good," said Tim, smiling. "I was hoping that

you could spend a little time with Emma and Caspian. Maybe show Emma a few of the methods you use at Heartland. I'm hoping that Emma can then pass on what she learns to the rest of my staff. I'm really eager to start using some alternative remedies. And, I think Emma would agree, Caspian is a perfect test subject."

Tim's suggestion was clearly as much of a surprise to Emma as it was to herself, Amy realized, noticing the stunned expression on Emma's face. Tim was waiting for her answer. "No problem, as long as it's OK with Emma," Amy said cautiously.

Tim looked across at Emma who, now that they had reached the yard, was fiddling with a strand of Mistral's mane. "That would be fine," she answered in a flat voice, without looking up.

"Glad to hear it," Tim said. Amy could see that her father didn't sense that there was anything wrong, but Amy had serious misgivings. *Emma has made it clear,* Amy thought, *that she wants as little to do with me as possible. How am I going to overcome that?*

✣

Helena was in the office when Amy and Tim arrived back at the yard. She came out when she heard them. "Productive session?" she asked Amy.

"Not one of my better ones," Amy replied honestly.

Helena gave her a sympathetic smile before turning to

Tim. "We're going to have to reorganize the yard schedule," she told him. "You had a phone call earlier about the delivery of the new horse. He's not arriving tomorrow morning now, but the day after."

Tim frowned briefly. "That's when we're going to be at the auction," he said.

Helena nodded. "It's OK. I've asked Sam to pick him up instead."

"That should work. Thanks." Tim smiled.

Helena pulled the office door shut. "Lou's cooking breakfast today," she told them. "So I hope you're feeling hungry."

🙟

Once they were sitting around the table, enjoying bacon, scrambled eggs, and sausages, Helena turned to Amy. "Why wasn't it one of your better sessions with Mistral?" she inquired.

"She kind of freaked out when I tried to lunge her," Amy admitted.

"I expect you're used to setbacks, though, from what Tim's told me about your work," Helena said.

Amy was about to describe some of the problem horses she had worked with when Lily spilled her cup of orange juice down her front. Lily's cries immediately distracted Helena, and Lou rushed to the sink to get a sponge. Amy then found herself thinking about her father's suggestion that she should help Emma with Caspian. She tried to figure out how she would approach the situation when Emma had been so unfriendly toward her. Amy thought their issues must be personal because Emma was very different when she was with Alex and Caro.

"What's wrong?" Lou asked, sitting down next to Amy and looking at her with concern.

Amy was suddenly aware of her father's eyes on her as well. "Nothing," she replied quickly. The last thing she wanted was to create problems at her father's stables.

Lou didn't look convinced, but she didn't push it. "I thought I'd come and take a look at Spirit and Mistral later this morning if that's OK," she suggested.

Amy's spirits lifted. "Of course it's OK," she replied happily. She was looking forward to spending some time with her sister.

          ❧

Amy had tethered Spirit to a ring in the yard and was just leading Mistral out when Lou emerged from Tim's office, a converted box stall at one end of the stable block.

Amy walked Mistral around in a circle, proud of her gleaming black coat and long silky mane, but Lou showed more interest in Spirit. She gave Mistral a vague pat before crossing over to the gelding. "He's beautiful," she enthused. "Helena's told me all about him."

"He's wonderful to ride," said Amy. "How about we go out together? You can ride Spirit and I'll ask Dad if I can take one of the other horses."

Spirit blew heavily on Lou's hair and she laughed. "OK. I'd like that," she said.

Amy felt pleased. Since Lou had only just started riding again, Amy savored the chance to go on the trails with her sister. "I'll go find Daddy and see if he can come, too."

When Amy tracked down her father in his office, she told him of their plans and asked him if she could take one of the other horses out.

"Sure," he replied. "You can take Lace if you like. I know Helena's not planning to ride today." He looked pleased to hear that Lou was going. "I'd love to come with you, but I've got mountains of paperwork to get through."

"We'll all go soon," Amy promised, and she headed back to Spirit's stall. She found Lou still petting the gelding and gave her the news.

"Great," Lou said. "I just need to change. Then we can head out." As she walked away, Mistral turned her head and watched her go. Amy noticed the mare's interest and was faintly surprised. She had never seen Mistral react that way before. She shrugged as she led the horse back into her stall. Maybe it had just been a coincidence.

❧

As Amy and Lou began their ride, Lou let out a contented sigh. "This is so nice," she declared happily, gazing out over the tree-lined fields.

"Should we head down to Fiddler's Creek?" Amy suggested. "I went there yesterday with Helena and Dad. It's a great ride."

"Sounds fine," said Lou easily. "Do you know, this is probably the best vacation I've ever had? Spending this time with Dad makes me feel like I'm catching up a little on the years we missed with him. And I'm really glad he married Helena — she's so open and friendly."

Amy was quiet as Lou talked about their father and his new family. She remembered that Lou had been close to their father until she was twelve years old, while Amy had known him for only the first few years of her life. The time she was spending at the ranch now was reminding her more and more of just how much she had missed out on. Seeing Tim and Helena with Lily made her nostalgic for memories she didn't even have.

"What do you think of Lily?" Lou asked, breaking in on Amy's thoughts.

"She's cute," Amy replied, remembering Lily's gurgling laughter when she was pushed on the swing. But

thinking of how Lily had reached for Lou made Amy realize again that she needed to spend more time with her
half sister. She told herself again that she should make
more of an effort during the rest of her stay.

"Are you OK to canter here?" she asked Lou, changing the subject as they turned into a long field that rose
up a slight hill.

Lou hesitated, and Amy sensed her anxiety.

"I promise you'll be fine," Amy told her reassuringly.
"Spirit's got an incredibly smooth pace, and you look
great. You're such a natural!"

Lou looked at Amy questioningly. "You really think
so?"

Amy thought about her sister's innate talent — and
what a shame it was that she'd lost her confidence. "Hey,
with our parents, we can't help but be great horse-
women," Amy teased, and she was happy to see Lou
smile in response. "Come on, I'll take the lead, OK?"
Amy said, and shortened her reins before nudging Lace
into a smooth trot. Once she could see that Lou was
posting in a relaxed way on Spirit, she sat deep into her
saddle and pushed Lace into a slow, controlled canter.
She heard Spirit change his stride behind her and, when
she glanced back over her shoulder, she saw Lou riding
easily — a big grin on her face.

Amy pulled Lace up at the top of the hill and looked at
the view spread out in front of her. Between the trees,

she could just make out glimpses of the snaking line that was Fiddler's Creek. The strong sunlight was glinting on the water, turning it into a silver ribbon.

Lou drew Spirit to a halt and patted him. "He's wonderful. I can't see why Dad needs you to work on him," she remarked to Amy.

"He's better on trail rides," Amy agreed. "It's in the ring that there's more of a problem. He loses all his enthusiasm there."

"What can you do to make a horse more eager?" Lou asked as they began to ride down toward the creek. "I can see how you could eventually gain a scared horse's confidence or get a disobedient horse to obey you, but how do you make a well-behaved horse enthusiastic?"

"I'm starting to wonder myself," Amy admitted. "I just hope that by spending lots of time with Spirit I can lessen the bond he's formed with Helena and start getting him to perform for other riders."

"Well, whatever faults he has in the ring, Helena's done a fantastic job with him," said Lou, stroking Spirit's proud, arched neck. "She must be pretty talented to get an unbacked horse to this standard within a year. Especially considering she had Lily to take care of."

"She's done no more than our own mom did when we were little," Amy was quick to interrupt. "Only she had the two of us then *and* her show-jumping career."

"Amy!" Lou looked surprised. "I wasn't even thinking

of it as a comparison between Helena and Mom. I was just commenting on the hard work she must have put in on Spirit, on top of everything else she had to do."

Amy chewed her lower lip. She was caught off guard by her outburst, too. She just couldn't help resenting Lou's clear admiration of Helena, when their own mother had done as much and more when she was alive.

❧

Tim was waiting for them in the yard when they got back. His eyes lit up at the sight of Lou in the saddle. "So, you enjoyed yourselves?" he asked.

"We had a great time!" Lou agreed enthusiastically as she dismounted and led Spirit into his stall.

It didn't take long for them to rub down the horses. Amy stood talking to Tim while Lou finished. As Lou stepped out of Spirit's stall, Mistral's head appeared over her door. Lou walked across to where Amy and Tim were waiting, and once again Amy noticed Mistral's eyes following her. Then, to Amy's amazement, Mistral lifted her head slightly and let out a long, deep nicker.

There was no doubt about it. Mistral was actually calling to Lou!

Chapter Six

꧁

"Of course I don't mind helping you with Mistral," said Lou to Amy later that afternoon, "although I don't see what I can do. And don't forget, Scott will be back in a couple of days and we'll be leaving then."

"That's fine," Amy told her. She crossed her fingers behind her back and hoped that two days would be long enough for her to work out why Mistral showed interest in Lou and no one else. She was sure it would provide her with the key to unlocking the mare's problems.

The door opened and Helena came out, carrying Lily. "Hello," she said as she noticed Amy sitting on the wicker chair. "We were just talking about you."

"You were?" asked Amy in surprise.

"Yes, we were just saying how much Amy likes to

ride, weren't we, Lily?" said Helena to the little girl who had her fingers tangled in her mother's curly hair.

Amy smiled at Lily. "Do you like horses, Lily?"

Lily turned her face into Helena's chest. "Come on, silly," Helena said, rubbing her back.

Amy felt a little frustrated, but she tried again. "Hey, Lily," she said softly.

Lily turned her head slightly and looked at Amy.

"Do you like horses?" Amy repeated.

Lily slowly nodded her head and then smiled brightly at Amy, who felt her heart skip. It was the first time since she had arrived that Lily had smiled at her. Maybe there was hope that she and her little sister would bond after all.

❧

When Amy woke the next morning she remembered her promise to help Emma with Caspian. She realized, with a sinking feeling, that she should try to approach her that day. Ordinarily, Amy enjoyed sharing her knowledge, but Emma didn't want her help, and that made the situation awkward.

Amy pulled her clothes on and tied back her hair before heading down to the yard. She thought at first that she was the only one awake and up but as she approached Caspian's stable she heard Emma's voice. She was talking to Caspian as she groomed him.

"Hi," said Amy, looking over the top of the door.

"Hello," Emma said brusquely, not even pausing in her long, sweeping strokes.

"You're here early," Amy commented.

"I've got a lot to do," Emma replied.

Despite Emma's cool welcome, Amy decided she'd give the conversation another try. "Do you want a hand with that?"

"I'm just finishing up," Emma declared, and packed the brisk brush into the grooming tray. She turned to face Amy. "I guess this means that you're here to *help* with Caspian."

"Dad was probably just thinking that I could show you some of the things we do at Heartland, that's all," Amy said.

Emma held her hands in the air and said in a sarcastic tone, "Believe me, we've all heard about the things you do at Heartland."

Amy could feel her cheeks growing warm. Before she could answer, Emma nodded toward the bottle she was holding. "Is that for Caspian?"

"It's a Bach Flower Remedy," Amy replied. "They are natural extracts of flowers and herbs. There are thirty-eight different remedies that can be used on their own or blended together." Amy took a deep breath and continued. "Since Caspian is so excitable, I thought we could try to restore his balance by using impatiens and aspen. They're particularly useful for calming nervous animals that anticipate threat the way Caspian does." She unscrewed the lid of the bottle. "You just need to put a few drops —"

"— into his water," Emma finished for her.

Amy looked at her with surprise.

"Lucky guess," Emma shrugged.

Amy held out the bottle. "You can also add it to his feed or use it with a pump and spray the air in the box stall," she told her quickly, trying to share as much as possible while she had Emma's attention. "You might try lavender on him, too. It's a great relaxant. You can mix it with some witch hazel and warm water, then wipe it over his face, neck, legs, and spine with a sponge. My dad picked up a bunch of supplies. They're on a shelf in the tack room."

"How long will it take before we see a difference?" Emma asked.

Amy tried not to look surprised at Emma's sudden show of interest. "Sometimes they work almost immediately. With luck, you'll start to see a small change in him by the end of the week," she replied. "But sometimes it's more gradual, and you're looking at months, not weeks." Amy paused, hearing a distant voice. She realized it was Lou calling her.

"Sorry," Amy apologized. "I should probably go."

"It's OK, I got the gist of it, anyway," Emma responded abruptly.

Amy sighed inwardly as she let herself out of the stall. Just as she had started to think that Emma's hostility was about to thaw, the stable hand had returned to her usual cold manner.

❧

Amy's expression brightened at the sight of her sister leaning over the stall door and looking at Mistral.

"She's very pretty," Lou observed as Amy joined her. "And big."

"She is, and you can tell by the way she moves that she would be incredible to ride," Amy replied.

Mistral snorted and edged backward until her tail touched the far wall. She stamped a back hoof and uneasily adjusted her stance.

"Does she always do that when people are around?" Lou frowned. Amy looked at her sister. She sensed that Lou was losing her nerve now that she had a better idea of Mistral's disposition.

"Dad says she's never shown any enjoyment in human company — until she saw you," Amy said reassuringly, as she slid back the bolt on the stable door.

"And you think there's something to that? Why me?" Lou asked.

Amy soothed Mistral before leading her from the stall. "Well, the only thing I've been able to come up with is that the couple of times you've been around Mistral, you've ignored her."

Lou half closed her eyes in concentration. "I guess so," she said slowly. "I was more interested in Spirit because I'd heard so much about him from Helena."

"Well, whatever the reason, it's given me an idea as to what we should try doing with her," said Amy as they made their way down to the ring. "I think that Mistral must have had some kind of bad experience in her past where she was pressured into doing something she wasn't ready for. I'm not sure what it could be because she isn't supposed to have had any real training yet. But if I'm right, then I think Mistral might be happier working with you."

"I don't understand." Lou ran her hand through her hair. "Surely the moment I start working with her she'll just see me as just another person pressuring her to perform."

"I've thought about that," Amy admitted. "But horses work on a different level from us. They react to what they see and hear, like we do, but they also react to what they *sense*. They rely a lot on instinct. I think Mistral senses you are different from everyone else she's met so far. Everyone who's been with her since she's arrived has been one hundred percent focused on the horses here and getting the best results out of them — and that includes me. But you're not. It was days before you even came down to the barn!"

Lou smiled ruefully. "I guess you're right," she acknowledged. "It's not that I didn't want to be with the horses, it's just that I was so intent on getting to know Lily and Helena."

"Exactly. For everyone else here, the horses are the priority," Amy finished.

Lou nodded her head slowly. "It does make sense, in a roundabout kind of way," she said dubiously. "But you'll have to tell me exactly what to do."

"Of course," Amy agreed. "And I'm hoping that I'll be working with her soon, too. We just need to convince her that being with us can be fun." As she walked to the edge of the ring, Amy thought about the secret hope that she hadn't shared with Lou — she hoped that by helping a strong, proud horse like Mistral, Lou would fully regain her confidence with horses at last.

❧

Lou had done join up back at Heartland, but it had always been with horses that were familiar with the technique. Judging by her sister's expression, Amy thought Lou must be nervous. Even from where she sat, Amy could see Lou's white knuckles as she clenched Mistral's lead rope. "Relax," Amy called across the ring. "Let her go and send her to the outside rail, just like you've done before."

Lou nodded and set her jaw in the determined expression that Amy often wore. As she sent Mistral to ringside, Helena and Tim approached from the ranch. The black mare shied slightly as they climbed onto the fence, and Lou instinctively took a step back. *Go on, Lou,* Amy willed her silently. She knew that it was important for Lou to deal with this on her own so that her confidence would grow. Lou hesitated for just a moment before retaking her stance and calling out sharply, "Mistral, move on!" The black horse snorted and immediately swerved back onto the track.

Tim and Helena sat on either side of Amy. "We thought we'd come down and see how things are progressing with Mistral," Tim told her. "Lou's got her going nicely."

It is true, Amy thought. Mistral was cantering steadily, with her neck arched and her tail raised. She was starting to relax and showed none of the tension of previous sessions.

"I've been telling Helena of my plan to start join up with my youngsters," Tim commented. "Can you explain to her what Lou's doing?"

"Sure." Amy shifted her position slightly and began to explain. "The purpose of joining up with a horse is to encourage it to *choose* to be with you, rather than trying to force it to work with you. Lou will drive Mistral away from her until she sees signs that the horse wants to join her. See?" She pointed at Mistral. "She's doing it now."

Helena watched as Mistral lowered her head, then opened and closed her mouth.

"Mistral's telling Lou that she no longer wants to run away from her," Amy went on. "In a moment, Lou will turn her shoulders so she's no longer in an aggressive stance, and she'll allow Mistral to come and join her in the center of the ring."

As Amy was speaking, Lou did exactly that, and Amy felt a wave of pride when Mistral walked across to her sister. Lou didn't look at the horse. Instead she walked to the perimeter of the ring and, without hesitation, Mistral followed her. Wherever Lou went, the mare followed, showing that she had put her trust and confidence in Lou and wanted to be her friend.

Amy felt a little choked with emotion. Seeing a horse joining up was always a powerful experience, but it meant even more to Amy to watch her sister make that connection.

"Wow," said Helena softly. "I've never seen anything like it."

Amy cleared her throat. "We use join up to begin a partnership with the horse that's based on trust, rather than domination."

As Helena nodded, Amy slipped from the fence and

walked across to Mistral. "Nice work, Lou." She smiled at her sister, whose cheeks were flushed.

"I can't believe I did it!" Lou exclaimed. "She was so good."

Lou quietly stroked Mistral's forehead while Amy clipped on the lunge line. "Now just a few laps on the lunge. Be nice and steady," Amy said. "She needs to feel your confidence, so make sure everything you do is smooth and controlled, OK?"

"What if she doesn't behave? What if she bucks or rears?" There was no mistaking the anxiety in Lou's voice.

"I'll be there right away," Amy promised. "But she won't. She trusts you. Just remember — reward good behavior, ignore bad behavior."

Lou nodded and raised the lunging whip to form a triangle between herself and Mistral. Then Lou called out in a firm voice for the mare to walk on.

Amy crossed her fingers and watched. To her amazement, Mistral walked calmly forward, her long black mane and tail blowing in the slight breeze.

"Trot," Lou called, giving the whip the slightest of flicks on the ground, and Mistral immediately sprang forward. She broke into a canter in the corner of the ring. Amy felt a knot of tension burn in her stomach, but Lou brought her back to a walk before sending her forward, once again, into a beautiful, balanced trot.

After ten minutes, Amy signaled to Lou to bring the session to an end and went over to congratulate her sister. They were soon joined by Helena and Tim.

"You were brilliant!" Tim exclaimed, spontaneously hugging Lou. "Well done, both of you! That's the most work we've ever gotten out of her," he enthused, turning to pat Mistral. The big black horse rolled her eyes and stepped backward. "Steady, girl," Tim soothed. "No doubt there's still a lot of work to be done," he said to Lou, "but you've made a tremendous breakthrough. I'd started to think about selling her, but seeing her move with that long stride makes me willing to take more time. She'll be worth it."

"That was great." Helena squeezed Lou's arm. Then she glanced at her watch. "I'd better get back to the house. I promised Caro I'd only be away for ten minutes! She's watching Lily for me."

"I'll come with you," Lou offered. "You don't need me to do anything else, do you, Amy?"

"No, thanks," Amy answered quietly, and took the lead rope from Lou. "I'd better walk Mistral back up to the yard and rub her down." She patted the mare's neck gently before clicking to her to walk on. Heading back to the barn, Amy was aware that she should feel more pleased with Lou's success. But she was struggling with an uncomfortable feeling — a feeling that she just didn't belong. She thought of Ty and Grandpa and everyone else at Heartland. When she was there, everything was so much easier. *Maybe I should have stayed at Heartland. I'm really needed there,* she thought.

Her eyes stung with tears, and feeling frustrated with herself, Amy blinked them away. She tried to think more positively as she rummaged in her pocket and pulled out a mint for Mistral. The mare cautiously lipped it off her hand. "That's a good girl." Amy stroked the horse's warm neck. "You did well today. The next step is for you to learn to put your trust in me, too."

🙟

Before schooling Spirit the next day, Amy spent a long time in his stall doing T-touch. She hoped that it would help him bond with her. As the gray horse turned to look at her through large brown eyes, he blew heavily. Amy smiled and he rested his head on her shoulder. "Hey, the idea's not to relax you so much you go to sleep!" she said, laughing and moving away.

Spirit's ears pricked up at the sound of hooves clattering in the yard. Amy looked out and saw Emma leading Caspian toward his stall. Her hair was in untidy strands around her face, and one side of her jodhpurs was caked in mud. She had obviously had a fall.

Amy rushed out. "Are you OK? Do you want me to take him for you?" she asked with concern.

Caspian had foam flecks on his chest and was pulling

against the reins, his nostrils raised and flaring. Emma didn't say anything. "What happened?" Amy persisted.

Emma rounded on her. "I've had enough of your help, thank you. Just let me handle my horse in my own way, OK? If your methods are so great, why aren't you getting anywhere with Spirit and Mistral? Just leave me alone!"

Leaving Amy standing with her mouth open in amazement, Emma tugged Caspian forward and slammed the door of his stall shut behind them.

Fine, Amy thought angrily. *If that's the way you want it, then that's all right with me.* She walked back into Spirit's stall, trying to suppress her anger. She felt more determined than ever to help Mistral and Spirit and prove that Heartland's methods, *her* methods, really did work. Deftly, she tacked up Spirit and led him down to the ring.

&

Although Spirit still wasn't the inspired horse that Amy had watched on the video, there was a slight improvement during his session. Usually, he tipped the top poles of his jumps, but this time he cleared every one with a few inches to spare.

"Well done!" Amy said, and patted his neck as they finished the circuit. She glanced at her watch. She had just enough time to get him back to his stall before taking Mistral to the ring to meet Lou.

❧

Lou was waiting in the center of the ring when Amy showed up with Mistral. The mare pricked her ears forward as soon as she noticed her. Amy handed the mare over to be lunged, hoping fervently that Mistral would have another stress-free session. It was essential if Amy's plan for her was going to work.

Amy watched Lou put the mare through various transitions on the lunging line. The horse went from a fluid canter to a trot before walking calmly around the track.

"That's great! Now try her on the other rein," Amy called.

Lou nodded and skillfully sent Mistral in the other direction. Amy looked at Lou's bright blue eyes, following each movement of the horse, and realized how much her sister's confidence was increasing.

"She's working well for you," Amy congratulated her sister as Lou brought Mistral to a halt.

"She's amazing," Lou said enthusiastically. "I'm going to miss working with her."

Amy frowned slightly, then suddenly realized what her sister meant. "Of course, Scott's coming back tomorrow!" Amy declared.

Lou nodded, her eyes lighting up. "I can't wait to see him," she admitted. "But I'm starting to understand how difficult it was for you to leave your work at Heartland.

After just two days, I already feel like it will be hard leaving Mistral. I'll be thinking about her progress and wondering what I could have done with her if I was here."

Amy felt a surge of delight. She had hoped that helping with the reluctant mare would help to restore her sister's confidence and love of horses. But it seemed Lou's work with Mistral had achieved even more. Lou was beginning to experience the bond that could develop between horse and healer.

"What you've done so far with Mistral is great," Amy said. "You've helped her understand that being with people can be good, not stressful. You're the only one who could have accomplished that. Now I think she's ready for the next step."

A look of curiosity passed across Lou's face. "What?" she asked curiously.

"You'll have to wait and see," Amy teased. "First of all, I need to make sure that she's comfortable with me lunging her, too."

Amy took over the lunging line and clicked to Mistral. The mare swiveled her ear toward the sound of Amy's voice. "Trot on," Amy called reassuringly, and watched with delight as, without a trace of anxiety, Mistral obeyed her command.

Amy worked Mistral for five minutes on each rein and then brought her back to the center of the ring. Between

Amy and Lou, they had spent hours with Mistral over the last couple of days, not just joining up with her but also doing T-touch and massage with essential oils. She was sure that the mare was now ready for the next stage in her training. Crossing her fingers, Amy walked over to the gate and collected the saddle and bridle she had brought down earlier.

"You're going to ride her?" Lou asked in surprise.

"Nope, I'm just going to introduce her to the tack and, as long as she's happy wearing it, then tomorrow I'll lunge her tacked up," Amy explained.

Mistral was looking at the tack with her ears back. "It's OK, girl," Amy said. She made sure that the girth was over the saddle and the stirrup irons were secured at the top of their leathers so that nothing could bang against Mistral's sides and give her a fright. Amy then lifted and placed the saddle gently onto Mistral's withers before running it down into position on her back. Mistral's muscles tensed, but she remained still as Amy slowly reached the girth around and fastened it into position.

"Good girl," Amy praised, and she gave Mistral a mint to crunch on. The mare lipped it off her palm, and Amy was pleased to see that she was showing none of the panic she exhibited when lunged for the first time. Mistral's face looked a little tense. Her nostrils were slightly flared, but there was something in her eyes that

Amy couldn't quite understand. The mare looked as if she knew what was going on. She didn't have the nervous look of a horse experiencing something new and strange.

Amy frowned.

"She's doing well, isn't she?" Lou commented.

"Almost too well," said Amy slowly.

"How can she do too well?" Lou asked in surprise. "Isn't she just responding to the work we've done with her? Showing she trusts us?"

"It would be nice to think so, but somehow I'm pretty sure that's not the case," Amy replied. She looked at Mistral, who was standing quietly. The behavior just didn't make sense — her dislike of people, her terrified reaction to being lunged, and now, her complete lack of surprise at a saddle.

Amy picked up the bridle and slowly passed the reins over the mare's head. As she placed the bit against Mistral's teeth, the horse immediately opened her mouth and accepted it.

"I thought so," Amy said.

"What?" Lou asked, puzzled.

"Whoever sold Mistral to Dad lied," Amy explained, frustration mounting in her voice. "He bought her unbacked, but she's worn a saddle and a bridle before. I'm sure of it."

Chapter Seven

"You actually managed to put a saddle and bridle on Mistral?" Tim asked, turning away from the fish on the grill to look at Amy and Lou in amazement.

"Yes," Amy nodded.

"And how did she react to that?" Tim seemed skeptical.

"To be honest, she acted like she'd done it all before," Amy told him.

"Amy's got an interesting theory," said Lou, setting a stack of plates on the table and then heading back inside.

Tim smiled encouragingly at Amy.

"I have a hunch," said Amy. "Well, more than than a hunch, really. I'm certain Mistral has been backed before. Do you mind if I use your office to look through her records this afternoon?"

"Of course you can. What are you hoping to find?" Tim asked with interest.

"I don't know yet, just any clue to Mistral's history, I guess," Amy replied.

"Well, I hope it helps," Tim said. "That would be an interesting development." Tim returned his focus to the grill, and Amy decided to head inside. As she reached the screen door, she looked into the kitchen and saw Helena standing with her arm around Lou's shoulders. The two of them were chatting and laughing, making silly faces at Lily. Almost in a daze, Amy took in the scene.

After a few moments she turned away and headed to the top paddock, where Mistral and Spirit were grazing along with Jinx and Lace. She leaned against the fence and rested her chin on the top rail.

Her thoughts drifted to the time her father had visited Heartland. Amy realized she was starting to understand a little of what her sister must have felt when she had struggled to bond with Tim during that visit, while Amy had gotten along with him so well. But here in Australia, things seemed different. She saw Lou earning her father's praise and being instantly accepted by Helena and Lily. Meanwhile, Amy felt increasingly alone. *Lou was able to spend so much more time with Dad when we were young. It's not surprising she's closer to him than I am,* Amy thought rather unhappily. She didn't feel any better, of course, when she considered the fact that Lily would have their father for the whole of her childhood, too.

She was so wrapped up in her thoughts that she didn't hear her father walk up behind her. "Lunch is ready," he said quietly.

"I'm not really hungry," Amy replied.

"Are you all right?" Tim asked.

"Sure," Amy said, forcing a smile onto her face as she slipped off the fence. "I'm just really eager to learn more about Mistral's background, that's all."

"OK. As long as you're sure," Tim told her. "I'd better get back to the barbecue before the fish are cremated," he joked. "See you later, Nancy Drew."

Amy watched him go, then made her way to the stables and let herself into his office. She figured one way of forgetting her problems was to concentrate on Mistral's.

The inside of the office was painted in neutral cream and coffee colors, and a huge potted palm tree flourished in one corner. One wall was taken up with filing cabinets, and Amy decided to begin her search with them. Each drawer was ordered by date, so she pulled out the bottom drawer of the end cabinet. Inside, everything was arranged alphabetically. Amy had no difficulty locating Mistral's file.

She took the slim green folder across to her father's desk and settled herself comfortably in his deep leather chair. Her attention was drawn to a collection of photographs grouped in one corner of the desk, and she interrupted her search to look at them. There was one of Tim and Helena on their wedding day. It was absolutely beautiful, and they looked very happy, but it still made Amy uneasy to see it. The only bride she had ever pictured her father with was her mother. She quickly glanced at the next photo and smiled to see a very young Lou, with her hair in braids, dressed in a school uniform. It must have been her first day at school in England, Amy realized. She ran her eye over the next few pictures — photos of horses her father had owned — and then came to the last frame, which contained two photos of Lily. There was one of Lily as a newborn, looking all red and wrinkled as she lay in Helena's arms, engulfed by a white blanket. In the next one she was a curly-headed toddler, asleep with a teddy bear, her tiny fingers clutching tightly to one paw.

Amy did a quick review of the frames and scanned the room for additional photos.

As she realized there weren't any more, Amy felt a sharp stab of pain. There was no photograph of her! She drew in a deep breath. *It doesn't matter,* she told herself. And, while it probably didn't make a difference to her dad, it mattered to her more deeply than she could put into words.

Quickly, she opened Mistral's file to try to focus on something else, but, as she leafed through the shipping bills and veterinary and insurance certificates, looking for an answer to Mistral's problems, one question lingered in her mind: *Why doesn't Dad have a photograph of me?*

She located the piece of paper she had been looking for, which was the bill of sale from Mistral's last yard. She reached for the phone and dialed the number written at the top of the page. A voice answered in Spanish, but the moment Amy spoke, the receptionist switched to heavily accented but excellent English. Amy briefly explained who she was and asked to speak to Mistral's previous owner.

"I'm so sorry, but he isn't here at the moment. Perhaps you would like to speak with the manager instead?"

"Thank you," Amy said politely, and waited until a deep male voice came onto the line.

As Amy began to describe the problems they were having with Mistral, the manager interrupted her brusquely. "You looked over the horse, and she was fine. You had a full veterinary inspection, which she passed. You cannot send her back."

"We don't want to send her back," said Amy quickly, trying to think of a sensitive way to phrase her question. "I was just trying to find out if she had any experience on your yard that might have upset her. Maybe there was an incident that could have made her afraid of people?"

"An incident?" the man said indignantly. "Are you trying to say that we mistreat our horses? We have the finest of reputations! The horse you have from us was one of our best. She was very good for us here. She had excellent prospects — clearing more than one and a half meters before she left."

"More than one and a half meters? But she was sold as unbacked!" Amy exclaimed. "It's on the bill of sale."

There was a long pause, and Amy wondered if they had been cut off, but then the manager spoke again. "She was sold as a youngster only," he said. "I have to go, I am a very busy man. I'm sorry, I cannot help you anymore."

There was a click as he hung up, but it didn't matter. He had given Amy the information she needed. She now knew why Mistral didn't like human company and didn't want to work. She had been backed and schooled at too young an age. The fact that she had been clearing one and a half meters indicated that Mistral had been forced to do too much too soon. It was, Amy thought, the equivalent of asking a small child to do algebra while still in nursery school. Considering this, Amy realized Mistral might have suffered something of a breakdown. It wasn't surprising that she now had a predisposition against people and being trained. She had allowed them to put a bridle and saddle on her, which meant that they were already moving in the right direction, but Mistral also needed to learn that training could be fun and easy.

Maybe then Amy could undo the damage that had been done.

❧

As Amy was putting the file away, her father's office phone began to ring. Amy hesitated, unsure whether she should answer it, then lifted the receiver. "Hello," she said.

"Hey. How are things?" a familiar voice asked.

"Ty!" Amy exclaimed. "How did you get this number?"

"I called the house," Ty explained. "They told me to try you here. So, you're doing some desk work?"

"Kind of. I've just discovered something about Mistral, the horse I'm working with." As Amy told Ty about her phone conversation, she felt a rush of happiness. *It was almost like being back at Heartland,* she thought, where she and Ty always discussed the horses' problems.

"So you want her to have fun?" Ty mused. "You could put a toy in her stall for a start."

"I was thinking that," Amy replied enthusiastically. "I know they're good for horses that get bored easily, but I thought that if Mistral were more interested in playing it might help her sense of curiosity. It might help her feel differently about the world around her." She paused for a moment, then continued. "It's so good to talk to you. How are things going back at home?"

"Good, thanks. Marnie's really enjoying herself, but she says she doesn't have 'city hands' anymore. She had to cut her nails." Ty laughed and Amy closed her eyes to concentrate on that sound. "Jack's been great. He's sharing the cooking with Marnie, and Lou would be impressed with his bookkeeping. Soraya is coming every day to help with the exercising. She said Sundance is keeping fit but missing you. Ben and I are doing just fine."

"Really?" Amy asked.

"Really," Ty replied firmly. "Now, how about you?"

Amy hesitated and then confided in Ty about her continuing struggle to fit in.

"I thought you said you were going to try to work on it," Ty said gently.

Amy sighed. "I've tried, but it's all so different from Heartland," she said. "I can't help feeling like everyone's interested in Lou and I'm just the invisible sister. I mean, Dad doesn't even have a photo of me on his desk." But even as she listed valid reasons for feeling isolated, she knew she hadn't made the same effort to fit in as her sister.

"These things don't happen overnight, Amy," Ty said reassuringly. "Being part of a new family is work. Maybe it's easier for Lou because she's older and can relate to Helena more, but I bet it takes effort for her, too. I know it will all work out. You've just got to give it time," he told her.

Amy agreed and said good-bye. As she hung up she realized that her time at the ranch was passing quickly. If she wasn't careful, she'd be going home nearly as much of a stranger to her new family as when she arrived.

🙚

Amy rummaged through the black bins in the tack room. There were mountains of spare leading reins, rubber reins, martingales, and halters, but she finally managed to find a green cylindrical canister. Feeling pleased, she went into the adjoining feed room, unscrewed the top of the canister, and filled it with some pony nuts.

She took the toy into Mistral's stall and encouraged her to sniff it before she put it down on the floor. The mare blew heavily through her nostrils at the toy, then ignored it completely. Amy felt a little disappointed, but she knew that it wasn't realistic to expect a horse like Mistral to immediately begin rolling it around on the floor. "The only way you can get the treats to fall out of the holes is by pushing the toy with your nose," Amy explained to the mare. "I want it empty by tomorrow morning," she added sternly. The she patted Mistral gently and slipped out the door.

🙚

By the time the evening meal was ready, Amy's stomach was rumbling from her missed lunch. She ate her way through the delicious stew that Tim had made and listened to Lou and Helena chat about their afternoon. They had taken Lily swimming in a local pool and spent some time in the gym while Lily played in the nursery.

Amy was fairly quiet throughout the meal until Tim turned to her. "Did you manage to find out anything about Mistral?" he asked interestedly.

Amy briefly told him what she had discovered.

"That's quite unbelievable," Tim said. "They had her jumping more than one and a half meters, you say?"

Amy nodded.

"I must phone Pete — he's my business partner in England. He'll be interested to know that our supplier isn't altogether forthcoming," Tim commented. "Well, I have to hand it to you, Amy. That kind of early exposure could easily cause Mistral's behavior."

Despite Tim's kind words, Amy felt unmoved by his praise. As soon as she could, she excused herself and escaped from the table. Although it had been foremost in her thoughts the entire meal, she couldn't bring herself to ask her father why he didn't have her photo on his desk with everyone around. She wasn't sure she wanted to hear her dad's explanation, but it was something she really needed to know.

❧

When Amy let herself into Mistral's box the next morning, the big black horse actually walked over to her and nuzzled her hand. Amazed, Amy could barely contain her delight. She quickly rustled a horse treat out of her pocket and fed it to the mare. She then slowly bent down and shook the toy she had left out the night before. It was empty! "Good girl! We'll fill your toy again tonight," Amy exclaimed.

She gave Mistral a thorough grooming and led her down to the ring. Lou hadn't arrived, so Amy spent half an hour lunging the mare fully tacked. The horse responded well, and Amy felt it was a sign that Mistral was finally learning to trust people again.

As she waited for Lou, she decided to have some fun. She sent Mistral out to the side of the ring and began the process of join up. Fairly quickly, the mare lowered her head and began to look as if she were chewing air. Amy turned her body away from Mistral to encourage her to come and join her.

The moment Amy sensed the horse behind her, she stepped away. Mistral followed and Amy moved faster. The mare followed her again, and Amy broke into a jog. Mistral quickened her pace until she was trotting after her. Amy stopped and rewarded her with a horse treat, then moved off again. She jogged around from spot to spot, with the mare chasing her, until finally she stopped, breathless and laughing, and gave the horse a last reward. For the first time, Mistral didn't stiffen as she patted her.

"She's coming along well," Lou called, walking over to greet them. "Pretty soon she'll be jumping through hoops."

"Very funny," Amy replied, elbowing her sister.

"I'm glad to see you looking happier," Lou commented. "You seemed kind of down last night. You hardly said a thing."

"I was really tired," Amy said noncommittally. She walked across to the fence to collect Mistral's tack. She didn't feel like bringing up the whole photo issue with Lou at that moment. "And I was thinking about what we should do with Mistral today," Amy said.

"What are you going to do with her now?" Lou asked.

Relieved that Lou had dropped the previous subject, Amy gave Lou a sly smile. "I think she's ready for me to sit on her."

A worried frown creased Lou's forehead. "I don't know, Amy, she's still unpredictable. Are you sure?"

Amy tried to remain patient. "I know what I'm doing," she said calmly. "All you have to do is boost me up so I can drape myself over Mistral's back. If she is frightened in any way, I'll slip off immediately without getting hurt."

Lou sighed and gave a nod. "But if she shows any sign of misbehaving, you'll slide right off, OK?"

"I promise," Amy said, tightening the chin strap on her hat before standing beside Mistral. She raised her left leg, and Lou gently boosted her over the saddle. Amy hung quietly over Mistral's back. The mare snorted nervously and took two steps back. Amy kept still and murmured, "Steady, girl. Steady."

Mistral blew long and loud out through her nostrils but stood still.

"What now?" Lou asked, barely raising her voice above a whisper. She held her hands in front of her, ready to come to Amy's rescue.

"Could you do a little bit of T-touch on her so that she relaxes?" Amy asked. "Then, when she does, you can lead her forward a few steps — just a few steps — then stop and reward her, then lead her a few steps more," Amy explained. Lou nodded and cautiously approached Mistral.

After a few minutes, Lou paused and said, "I'm going to lead her forward now."

Mistral took three steps before Lou stopped and patted her gently.

"Go farther now. I think she's going to be all right," Amy said quietly.

As Lou began to walk around the ring, Amy carefully inched her leg over Mistral's quarters and slowly sat up in the saddle. Mistral swiveled one ear back toward her but kept the other pricked forward happily. After they

had completed one circuit of the ring, Lou halted and
Amy gently dismounted.

"Wow!" Lou exclaimed in delight. "I can't believe that
we've made so much progress before I have to go away!"

"I know," Amy said. She nodded and rubbed the mare
gently between the eyes. "You're doing really well, girl,"
she told Mistral, and dropped a kiss on her satiny nose.

❧

When Amy led Spirit down to the jumping arena
later that day, she was still glowing from her success
with Mistral. She began to warm up Spirit by asking
him to trot around the perimeter of the ring. Soon she
was sure that the horse was picking up on some of her
happiness. His paces were smoother and more confident
and, as Amy pointed him toward the first jump, she felt
him give a rush of pleasure for the first time. His paces
became elevated, his neck arched proudly, and he
pushed eagerly against the bit.

"OK, boy, it's just you and me," she whispered.

Spirit collected himself and flew over the first jump as
if he had wings. Amy laughed aloud at his enthusiasm.
As she concentrated on the second jump, the gray suddenly missed his stride. Spirit called out loudly. Amy cir-
cled to see what had distracted him. She saw that
Helena and Lou were walking along the path between
the arena and the ranch. Amy tried to collect Spirit, but

his stride was uneven. Circling again, Amy tried to help Spirit find his pace. She pointed him at the fence once more, but he sped up at the last minute and lost his footing. Amy fell over his neck as he crashed through the fence, poles flying everywhere.

Amy was shaking as she pushed herself against Spirit's neck to sit back up in the saddle. Annoyed and frustrated, she knew she wouldn't regain the momentum she had lost. She dismounted and checked Spirit's legs, making sure he hadn't injured himself. Despondency crept over her as she realized that she had completely underestimated the bond between Spirit and Helena. She couldn't remember seeing a horse respond so strongly to another person before.

"Oh, Amy, I'm so sorry," Helena said, hurrying toward the ring. "We had just come back from taking Lily for a walk. I didn't think what might happen if you were with Spirit."

"It's fine," said Amy shortly, trying hard not to show her frustration but knowing that she wasn't succeeding. Helena watched from outside the ring. Amy noticed her stunned expression, but Amy refused to say anything to make her feel better. She could only think about her own work with Spirit. If she *had* made a breakthrough with the horse, then Helena had effectively ruined it all. Helena turned away as Amy started to lead the gelding to the stable.

"Amy?" Lou called after her as she walked away. Amy could see her sister's puzzled frown, but she didn't care.

Then a window at the back of the ranch house suddenly opened, and Tim stuck out his head.

"Hey!" he called to Lou. "You have a visitor who's very eager to see you!"

Lou's concerned expression was replaced with one of joy as she realized who her father meant. "Scott's back!" she said to Helena, and they headed up to the house.

❧

Just as Amy was turning the handle of her bedroom door, Lou came up the stairs. "I'm just going to give Lily her bath. Will you help me?" she asked Amy.

"Actually, Lou, I was planning to go to bed early tonight. I've got to be up early tomorrow," Amy said.

"Oh, come on, Amy, who are you trying to kid?" Lou replied, taking Amy by surprise. "What is wrong with you? You don't try and join in, you don't want to have anything to do with Lily, and you're icy with Helena when all she tries to do is make you feel like part of the family. You don't even seem comfortable with Dad or me. I just don't understand why you're being like this."

Amy's mouth dropped open. Of all people, she never would have imagined Lou could be so insensitive. "Oh, forget it," Amy said, feeling a surge of frustration. "It's been so easy for you. I should have known you wouldn't understand."

"What's that supposed to mean?" Lou snapped.

"I thought you might have sympathized," Amy continued, "considering how left out you felt when Dad came to stay with us at Heartland!"

There was a long pause. Both sisters stared at each other. "Are you saying that you feel like you don't fit in?" Lou asked, looking bewildered.

"Yes, Lou, that's exactly how I feel, but don't worry, because it won't be long before I'm back at Heartland, where I'm actually needed!" Amy retorted, storming into her bedroom and slamming the door behind her.

Chapter Eight

❧

With trembling fingers, Amy pressed Ty's number into the phone. He answered it on the third ring. "Amy?" he questioned, sounding surprised.

"Hi, how are you?" Amy asked, aware that her voice was shaking.

"Everything's good here," Ty told her. "At least I think it is. It's not even six yet. What's going on?"

Amy suddenly realized that, with the time difference, she was calling in the middle of the night. Still, she was comforted by the sound of concern in Ty's voice. He understood her so well. "Oh, Ty. I'm sorry for calling so early, but things are a mess here. I'm starting to wish I hadn't come," she admitted, lying back on her bed and staring up at the ceiling. "At least if I'd stayed at home I would have been useful. I'd have known what to do and how to do it."

"Amy, what are you talking about?" Ty asked. "What happened?"

"I haven't managed to do anything right since I came here. I'm not having much luck with the horses, and it's even worse on the people side of things," Amy confessed. "I just can't get my footing here. Dad and Helena think Lou is fantastic, and Lily loves her, too, and always calls for her, but doesn't want to have anything to do with me. And Lou doesn't understand how I feel. She thinks everyone has gone out of their way to be nice to me."

As she took a breath, Ty interrupted. "Hey, Amy, this isn't like you."

"What do you mean?" Amy asked defensively. She had been expecting Ty to support her.

"Well, you usually love to join in and get involved. It's not like you to isolate yourself. And you're usually up for a challenge, too."

"But I feel so left out here," Amy said. "And the horses are more of a challenge than I bargained for. I've worked with them every day, and Spirit hasn't improved at all."

"Well, I'm afraid you won't want to hear this, but the horses should be the least of your worries. Your father's family will always be part of your life. You need to spend time with them," Ty insisted.

Amy had to admit it was probably true. "Horses are just so much easier," she said quietly.

Ty laughed, then his voice became gentle. "Amy, you can't build your place in the family just by being effective with your dad's horses. It's going to take more. I think that you went to Australia with the wrong expectations. Don't get me wrong, but it's like you expected everyone out there to see you and treat you the same way that we do at Heartland. But to them you're Lily's big sister and Tim's daughter. Maybe if you tried seeing yourself that way, you might find it easier to fit in."

Amy took a while to think over what Ty was saying. It wasn't what she'd wanted to hear, but she had a feeling he might be right.

Ty must have guessed that she was struggling with her emotions because he added quietly, "I'm sorry if I sounded harsh, but I wanted to be honest. I want you to get to know Tim's family, because I'm certain they'll love knowing you. You have a lot to offer. But, in this case, you probably have to do it on their terms."

Amy took a deep breath, letting his words sink in. "Thanks, Ty," she said in a small voice. "You're probably right, but it's just so hard for me." She sighed. "You should go back to sleep. Give my love to Grandpa."

"I will," Ty promised. "I'll be thinking about you. Take care."

Amy lay on her bed, her head buried in her arms. She

thought over what Ty had said, knowing she needed to try harder. But she was so tired that, before long, she was sound asleep.

When Amy walked up from the stables the following morning, she was surprised to see Scott stowing bags in the back of a green Jeep.

"I rented it for the week," he explained.

"I didn't think you'd be leaving this early," said Amy, looking around for Lou. She knew she couldn't let her sister leave without making up with her first.

"We've got a lot of driving to do. We're heading out to Alice Springs, then on to visit Uluru."

"Uluru?" Amy frowned.

"It's the Aboriginal name for Ayers Rock. Apparently it means great pebble. I've been reading my guidebook," Scott explained with a grin.

A movement on the veranda caught Amy's eye, and she turned to see Lou struggling with two hiking back-packs. "Here," Amy said, jogging across to help.

"Thanks," said Lou glancing up at her.

Amy read the expression in her eyes and sensed that Lou wanted to put their argument to rest as much as she did. "I'm sorry," said Amy softly. "I thought about it, and I guess I haven't made much of an effort."

"I'm sorry, too." Lou smiled. "I should have realized

you were struggling with things. It's perfectly under-
standable. Maybe while I'm gone you'll be able to work
things out. Get to know Lily. She's your sister as much
as mine, and she'll love you, I know she will. And just try
to relax with Helena. She doesn't want to be a second
mother to us, just a friend. You know what?" Lou looked
thoughtful. "I think Mom would have liked her."

Amy nodded her head before shouldering the backpack and walking across to the Jeep with Lou. "I spoke
with Ty last night, and he told me to stop thinking of myself as Heartland's Amy and start seeing myself as part
of the family instead."

"That's good advice," Lou said, nodding as she placed
her bag in the back of the Jeep.

"What is?" Scott asked, tipping his sunglasses down
onto the bridge of his nose and peering over at them.

"Being nice to sisters!" Lou laughed as she and Amy
hugged each other. Amy smiled at Lou, appreciating that
her sister had not explained the situation to Scott.

"I said good-bye to Dad, Helena, and Lily when you
were down on the yard," Lou told Amy. "They've gone
to an auction with Pat. Helena asked me to tell you that
there are fresh-baked muffins in the oven for your
breakfast."

Scott started the engine, and Lou pulled herself into
the passenger seat.

"Have a great time," Amy called through the window.

"See you next week!" Lou replied, and waved as the Jeep rolled away.

Fighting the sudden surge of loneliness that swept over her, Amy waved back until her sister had disappeared from sight.

❦

Amy figured that the best thing she could do was go for a long ride on Spirit. She needed time to mull over Lou's words. Deciding she could have breakfast later, she headed back down to the yard. Emma was outside Caspian's stall, talking to Caro. Amy couldn't help but overhear Emma complaining about having to pick up a horse from the airport with Sam.

"I'd love to help you, but I need to exercise Jupiter this morning," said Caro as she stroked the nose of the roan horse that stood in the box next door to Caspian.

Emma sighed. "It's OK, I promised Tim I'd do it. It's just that I would really like to put in a session with Caspian now that the schooling ring's free."

Amy thought quickly. She could put off her ride on Spirit. If she offered to pick up the horse, Emma might reconsider her feelings about her. It was worth a try. "I don't mind going if you're busy," she volunteered.

Emma turned around and gazed at Amy. "Well, if you're sure," she said after a pause. "Sam's expecting to meet me outside the house in a couple of minutes."

"I'll go now, then," Amy told her, and as she turned to retrace her footsteps, she thought she heard Emma mumble "Thank you" in a low voice.

❧

Sam was just pulling up outside the house as Amy arrived. He looked surprised when she climbed in beside him, but didn't say anything. "I offered to come instead of Emma," she explained.

Sam peered at her for a moment with his sharp blue eyes. Then he grunted and tugged his wide-brimmed hat farther down over his face. He let out the clutch, and the trailer pulled away down the long, sweeping driveway.

Amy leaned her forehead against the glass and looked out over the pastures. She was glad to be going with Sam. Since he never felt the need to make conversation, she would be able to sort through her thoughts in peace. Being away from the ranch, even for a couple of hours, would do her good, she realized. It would give her the distance she needed to put her worries into perspective.

❧

It took an hour to get to the small local airport. During the trip, Amy turned over in her mind everything that Ty and Lou had said to her. The more she considered their advice, the more she felt her guilt about forging a relationship with Helena disappear. Lou's words kept ringing in her ears: *Mom would have liked Helena.* Amy realized Lou was right. Helena and her mom would have had a lot in common. She had tried to deny this — pitting the two against each other in her mind. She had believed she couldn't be loyal to the memory of her mother and be open to Helena, too. But now Amy understood nothing would challenge the bond between her and her mother. With that last thought, Amy felt the final barrier in her mind lift.

❧

Sam drove around to the loading dock and, for the first time in the journey, he spoke to Amy. "Wait here while I go and take care of the paperwork," he said quietly.

Amy waited patiently until Sam returned.

"There." He nodded his head.

Following his gaze, Amy saw a dun-colored horse being walked along a chain-link fence. Even from a distance, Amy could see that the horse was frightened. His movements were stiff and unyielding and he repeatedly tossed his head.

She followed Sam over to the groom. "Sorrel tripped and skidded down the ramp when we brought him off the plane," the man explained. "The vet's checked him over and he's fine, but it unsettled him a little."

Amy ran her eyes over the gelding. He was typical of

many of the horses that her father bought — rough and unconditioned, but with good conformation that an experienced horseman could recognize. "We'll take him from here," said Sam. He looked across at Amy. "You can lead him."

Amy took the lead rope and spoke gently to the horse. She didn't like the closed expression on his face; she had come across it before with frightened horses. They would shut themselves off from the outside world and focus only on their fear.

Amy began to lead Sorrel over to the trailer as Sam brought down the ramp. The horse skittered away nervously, and Amy began to doubt that he would load easily.

"Bring him on," Sam told her.

Amy clicked softly and began to walk forward. She felt a surge of relief as he followed her. The moment his hooves touched the ramp, however, he dug his toes in and refused to go any farther. "Come on, boy," Amy encouraged, but when she took another step, he stumbled backward, his hocks buckling beneath him. Amy steadied herself and looked over at Sam, who rolled his eyes in exasperation.

"This one'll need a tranquilizer. No question," he said, taking a step toward the truck.

"Wait. Can I try something first?" Amy asked.

Sam shrugged and gave her a nod.

Amy rested her fingers at the base of Sorrel's forelock. She kept her fingers still for a moment so that he could adjust to her touch before she began to work in slow circles. She varied her touch, sometimes pressing her fingers down with a steady pressure and sometimes making circular movements. Eventually, Sorrel began to lower his head and breathe deeply. Amy walked a few steps forward but she felt Sorrel tense the moment he reached the ramp. "May I borrow your bandanna, please?" Amy asked Sam.

Sam looked at her and slowly shook his head as if she had made a ridiculous request, but he pulled the red bandanna off and handed it to Amy. She very gently placed it over Sorrel's eyes so that he couldn't see. "Now you have to depend on me," she whispered to him with a pat. "Walk on, there's a good boy. Trust me, you'll be OK."

Sorrel's ears were pricked toward the sound of Amy's voice, and as she urged him up onto the ramp he took four shaky steps and entered the trailer. "Good boy," Amy praised him, and carefully removed the bandanna.

Sam brought up the ramp behind them, and Amy smiled as she heard him mutter, "Well, I never."

She secured Sorrel and gave him some words of encouragement before slipping out the side door and joining Sam.

"Well done," he said gruffly before turning on the radio to dissuade further conversation.

Amy smiled to herself. She somehow felt the success with Sorrel and Sam's grudging praise were an omen for the remainder of her stay. She believed it was a sign that things were going to change for the better — and she was determined that this time she was going to make things work.

❧

There was a welcome committee at the yard when Amy and Sam arrived. Tim was waiting, along with Pat, Alex, and Caro. Emma walked up leading Caspian.

"We're always eager to see the new arrivals." Caro grinned as she helped Amy lower the ramp.

Sorrel was going to be Alex's horse, so as soon as the trailer was open, he went inside. Sorrel had calmed down during the journey and he backed obediently down the ramp, but Tim's sharp eyes noticed the dry sweat on his coat.

Sam explained how Amy had calmed Sorrel and covered his eyes to lead him into the trailer. "I didn't think we were going to get that horse in without heavy sedation and a forklift," he admitted.

Tim looked across at Amy. "What made you think of that?" he asked.

Aware that everyone was listening, Amy felt shy as she replied. "Well, since his eyes were covered, he had to trust me completely and wasn't distracted by any of his surroundings." She shrugged. "It's what they did during the fire in *Black Beauty*, so I thought I'd give it a try."

Tim laughed. "I'm glad you did," he said proudly. "Thanks for going."

He moved in closer to examine the horse, and as he did, Amy noticed the sullen expression on Emma's face. *Of course*, Amy thought. *Emma was supposed to be the one to pick up Sorrel. Now she thinks that I've tried to show her up.*

Emma turned on her heel and walked off, Caspian trailing behind. Amy made up her mind to set things straight with the stable hand. As soon as she could, Amy left the group and went in search of Emma. She found her in the jumping arena, cantering Caspian in circles. Caspian was frothing at the bit and trying to go sideways rather than straight. Amy could see that he was full of tension that he'd picked up from Emma. He was craning his neck and fighting the bit.

Emma set him at the first jump. Caspian seemed to settle down slightly, and he cleared it well. But as Emma swung him around to face the parallel bars, Amy fell into her line of vision. Amy watched as Emma's eyes dropped. Caspian immediately missed his stride and brought down the bars.

Emma tightened her reins and sent him on to the double, which he refused. Looking furious, Emma made Caspian circle tightly and take the jump again. Again he balked. Amy couldn't bear to watch Caspian become any more upset. She suspected Emma would never usually jump him like this, and she was afraid of how it would set back Caspian's progress.

Amy took a deep breath. She knew that challenging Emma would only antagonize her, but Caspian was becoming increasingly distressed. She quickly crossed the arena. Emma was attempting the jump for the third time. On this approach, Caspian swerved away, almost sending Emma over his shoulder as he dodged the standard.

"I think he's picking up on your tension," Amy said, standing in the center of the ring. "Do you mind if I try to calm him down a little bit for you?"

Without waiting for an answer she stepped forward and placed her hand gently on Caspian's forehead. Caspian backed away, his eyes rolling. Amy chose a different point and, speaking soothingly to the horse, began to move her fingers in a circular motion. Amy was concentrating so much on Caspian that she didn't notice that Emma had dismounted until the girl was facing her.

Emma's face was white except for two bright red patches on her cheeks. She spoke in a voice trembling with fury. "I'm sick of this. You come over here so full of yourself, thinking you're above us all with your alternative methods and theories," she snapped. "You're not the only one who can get the best out of horses, you know, even if you think you are. Your dad wouldn't have me here if I didn't get good results."

Amy felt stunned. All she had been trying to do was help. As she took a breath to defend herself, Emma continued. "All you've done since you came here is take over. I'm really interested in alternative methods, but I'd like to have used them on Caspian without you constantly butting in and taking control — not to mention taking all the credit. Did you ever think of that? Of course not! Because you never consider other people's feelings." She gave a short, bitter laugh. "Well, if you're so much better than me, you can have Caspian!" Emma flung the reins into Amy's hands and began stalking away across the ring. She then spun on her heel and pointed her finger. "You might know what you're doing around horses, but trust me, you've got a lot to learn when it comes to handling people!"

Chapter Nine

❧

Amy walked Caspian around to cool him off before taking him back to his stall. She rubbed him down, wondering all the while how she could possibly work things out with Emma. A shadow fell across the doorway, and Amy looked up to see Emma, fiddling nervously with the lead rope that was hanging over the door.

"I'm sorry," Amy and Emma both said at the same time, then half smiled at each other.

"I shouldn't have yelled at you like that," Emma apologized. "And I want you to know that I would never usually treat Caspian that way. I guess I let my own problems cloud my judgment. He deserves better." She let herself into the box, and Caspian nickered softly before moving across to her. Emma reached out her hand, and he nibbled on her fingers.

"I'm sorry, too," said Amy. "I guess I've been a bit insensitive at times."

Emma raised an eyebrow questioningly.

"I hadn't thought about how rude it was, the way I took over with Caspian when I first met you," Amy explained.

"I would have preferred it if you'd explained to me that he was frightened and suggested that I walk out in front of him," Emma admitted. "And explained why."

"I know. That's what I should have done," Amy replied sincerely, thinking things through. "It's so different at Heartland, and I acted just like I would have there."

Emma nodded. "Well, the good news is that there's been a definite change in Caspian over the last few days," she said more brightly. "He's not spooking at everything the way he was, and he's not getting overexcited whenever I ask him to go faster than a trot."

"That's good to hear," Amy said, grateful that Emma had changed the subject.

"But I've probably undone all the good work now," Emma said, looking miserable.

"Of course you haven't," Amy said quickly. "Just spend some time with him now to reassure him, keep applying the flower remedies, and I'm sure he'll continue to improve."

"Do you think so?" Emma asked hopefully. "I think he has so much potential. I really want him to be able to relax and find his rhythm." She paused and looked a little awkward. "Can you show me how to do that massage?" she asked shyly. "I've tried to do it out of a book, but I'm not hitting the right spots because Caspian always pulls away."

Amy gave Emma a small smile. "Sometimes horses respond better to massage in one area than others. It's a little like using herbs. They often choose the ones that they want you to use, if you offer them a selection," Amy told her.

"Really?" Emma looked surprised.

Amy nodded and felt a flood of exhilaration; she was finally having a conversation with Emma — and a good one at that. She continued to tell Emma the basics of herbs and T-touch. As she came to a stopping point, she looked at Emma. She was impressed with her interest and her natural sense of Heartland's methods. "I'm really sorry if you feel I've tried to take over since I got here," Amy said, watching as Emma began to brush some powdered lavender into Caspian's coat.

"I knew deep down that you weren't trying to be controlling," Emma admitted. "It's just that Tim had gone on and on about how you always get such great results from horses and how I'd be able to learn a lot from you. I guess I was pretty intimidated. I think I didn't *want* to like you."

"Well, I'll be the first to tell you that there's nothing intimidating about me." Amy smiled.

Emma shook her head. "That's the funny part. He also said how kind and generous you are. I think Tim thought we'd get along really well."

Amy took a brush to work on Caspian's other side. "My dad said that about me?" Amy asked, her gray eyes still wide with surprise.

"Yeah. Why are you so surprised?" Emma asked curiously.

Amy sighed. "I guess it's because I've had a hard time finding my place here," she admitted.

Emma looked surprised.

Amy continued moving the brush in long, firm strokes. "It's so different from being at home," she went on. "There's always something that needs to be done at Heartland. But here, there's really nothing for me to do besides working with Mistral and Spirit."

"But surely you didn't come just to work on your dad's yard," Emma pointed out. "Didn't you come to spend time with him and Helena and your new sister?"

"I'm beginning to realize that now," Amy agreed. "You know, since I got here, I've been trying to fit in in the same way I do at Heartland, but that's not really who I am here. So now I've decided that before I leave I'm going to make a real effort to try to become part of my new family." She paused, surprised by how much she was sharing with Emma. "The problem is, I don't really know how to start."

Emma looked thoughtful. "I understand how you feel. It must be kind of awkward, but I'm sure everything will work out before you leave." She gave Amy a reassuring smile.

"I hope so," Amy said, and as she smiled back, she realized that they had embarked upon the beginning of an unexpected friendship.

❧

Later that evening, Amy prepared feeds for Spirit and Mistral before tracking down Emma in the tack room. She was piecing a bridle back together and looked up as Amy walked in.

"I've put together some more flower remedies for you," Amy said, holding out a bottle.

"Thanks." Emma took the bottle and placed it carefully on the shelf. "I've been thinking, and I have an idea that might help you," she said thoughtfully.

"Really?" Amy felt pleased that Emma was trying so hard to be friendly.

Emma nodded.

"I'm all ears," Amy replied.

❧

During dinner, Amy noticed that conversation was a little strained. She felt awful as she remembered the way she had snapped at Helena when her stepmother had disturbed her session with Spirit. Amy knew it had been unintentional, but she had not been able to conceal her frustration at the time. Helena was obviously doing everything possible not to ask about the gelding's progress, and her brown eyes widened with astonishment when Amy brought up the subject by asking what she had enjoyed most about riding him.

Helena thought for a second before her face broke into a wistful smile. "It was the way he wanted to give me his all. It never felt like he was just obeying me because I was the one in control. It felt like we were a team, and he wanted to contribute one hundred percent to what we were doing."

Amy sighed. "I'm beginning to think Spirit is a one-woman horse. He's working well enough for me, but not in the way you're describing," she confessed.

"He didn't for me, either, in the early days. It was actually not until after his illness that we really bonded," said Helena.

"His illness?" Amy frowned.

"Yes, I'll never forget that night. The vet couldn't get out to us, and we thought we were going to lose Spirit to a bad bout of colic," Tim explained.

"I spent all night in his box, nursing him — *willing* him to pull through," said Helena with a faraway look in her eyes. "We were afraid he wasn't going to make it. It was terrible to see him suffering. But I was determined not to give up on him. When he was finally fit and well again, it felt like we had been through a battle together."

"I know that feeling. I sometimes spend whole nights with horses back home, too," Amy said, beginning to realize that she might have more in common with Helena than she had thought.

The phone rang and Helena smiled apologetically as she went to answer it. Amy ate a mouthful of rice but didn't really taste it. She was mulling over what Helena had told her. Now she could understand the level of devotion that Spirit had given to Helena. Helena had earned it after all her care. She suddenly felt a great empathy with the beautiful gelding. *I can't expect him not to want to be with Helena anymore. I just want him to give me a little of himself, too,* Amy thought. Immediately Amy felt a churning in her stomach as she realized that her situation wasn't so different from Spirit's. She could apply the same thinking to her own situation with Helena. For the first time, she realized how it must feel for Helena, who was only trying to earn her trust as a friend, but having to fight against Amy's devotion to her mother.

"Penny for your thoughts," Tim asked gently.

Amy glanced up and met his concerned gaze. "I'm just working through a few ideas," she smiled, realizing that all she had been doing for the last few minutes was pushing food around her plate.

Helena came back to the table, and Amy suddenly remembered Emma's suggestion from earlier. Now was as good a time as any to put her advice to work. "I hear it's your anniversary tomorrow. Do you have any plans yet?" she asked tentatively.

Tim looked a little surprised. "Oh, I don't think so. We didn't want to go out and leave you on your own — not with Lou away, too," he told her.

"No, no, you have to go out!" Amy exclaimed. "You need to celebrate. I'll be fine, and it's not like you get to go out often."

"I don't know that we'd be able to get a babysitter at such short notice," Helena said as she began to clear the table.

"You don't have to worry about that," Amy said quickly. "I'll look after Lily. I'd love to. I haven't spent much time with her since I've been here, and it would give us a chance to get to know each other."

Tim and Helena looked at each other. "If you're sure you don't mind . . ." Helena said slowly.

"I'm more than sure," Amy replied firmly.

&

Amy met up with Emma in the schooling ring the next day and gave the thumbs-up sign in response to her raised eyebrows. "I'm on official babysitting duty tonight!" Amy told her.

"Great news!" Emma said, looking pleased. She was

sitting lightly on Caspian in the center of the ring. He was resting his hind leg and appeared very relaxed.

"He's looking good," Amy observed happily.

"He is, isn't he?" Emma sounded proud.

"Can I see how he's going?" Amy suggested.

Emma squeezed him forward onto the track and sent him into a steady trot. She put him through all the paces and ended up by doing a shoulder-in. Throughout it all, Caspian kept a perfect balance and was relaxed and obedient. Finally, Emma brought him to a halt and dismounted. Her cheeks were flushed, and Amy smiled to see her so happy.

"He's so much more relaxed, Amy," Emma told her. "I never thought I'd see him like this."

"He's really coming along," Amy replied. A thought struck her. "Now that you don't have to spend so much time concentrating on Caspian, I wonder if you could ride Spirit for me?"

"Sure." Emma looked at Amy quizzically. "But why?"

"He needs to get used to other riders, too," Amy explained, but she didn't mention that Spirit had still not shown any sign of breaking his bond with Helena.

Emma was too concerned with making a fuss over Caspian to ask any more questions. Amy felt a rush of delight as she watched Emma trot figure eights on Caspian, and she hoped that her own breakthrough with Spirit would not be too far in the future.

❧

Mistral was looking out over her door when Amy walked back up to the yard. As soon as she saw Amy, she let out a long, low whinny. Amy stopped and stared. Mistral had never called out to her before. She felt it boded well for their training session.

She tacked Mistral up before leading her out and slowly mounting her. Knowing the mare's history made Amy cautious, but she believed a measured approach to training would allow the mare to gain full confidence in her abilities — and in her riders. Mistral shifted her hindquarters slightly when Amy put her weight in the saddle, but that was all. Amy squeezed her forward and Mistral obediently walked on. Amy rode her into the schooling ring, where Emma was waiting with Caspian. "Will you give me a lead?" Amy called. "I'm sure that following another horse will really help Mistral. Just take a steady pace."

Emma nodded and rode Caspian in front of Mistral. They completed two circuits at a brisk trot and then Amy called for Emma to canter. In the next corner, Emma sat deep into her saddle and sent Caspian into a smooth canter, which Mistral followed. Amy thought Mistral's stride felt like silk. After one circuit, they slowed back to a walk and let the horses stretch their necks. As they did, there was the sound of someone clapping, and they noticed Tim standing by the fence. "Impressive!" he called, crossing over to them. "They're both doing really well!" he exclaimed in delight. He gave Caspian a pat and looked up at Emma. "You've been working really hard. I can't believe how steady he's become. I couldn't have done any better with him myself."

"It's all thanks to the remedies Amy gave me," Emma said, her cheeks turning red.

"No, it isn't," Amy put in quickly. "They're only effective when combined with sympathetic handling. You've never given up on him, that's what's really brought him through."

"And as for Mistral, she's unrecognizable," Tim remarked, turning his gaze on Amy. "What you've done with her is amazing."

"Thanks, Dad." Amy felt a rush of happiness.

"Do you mind if I try her out?" Tim asked.

Amy hesitated. She wondered if it would be a little too much, too soon for Mistral. But then, she realized, her father knew what he was doing. "Sure," she said, slipping down and helping him adjust the stirrup leathers.

Tim mounted lightly and squeezed Mistral forward. Mistral laid her ears back at first and looked uncertain at leaving Amy and Caspian. But Tim maintained the pressure behind the girth and Mistral obediently stepped away. Amy watched her father's fluid movements in the saddle as he rode Mistral. He trotted her in a serpentine, applied a half halt, and then sent her forward into a controlled canter.

"I could watch your dad ride all day," Emma commented as they witnessed his expert handling of Mistral.

Amy nodded and felt a surge of pride. "My dad," she said softly.

&

"Our cell phone numbers are written down here," Helena said, showing Amy. "She's already in her pajamas. If she's thirsty, juice is in the refrigerator. Make sure to turn her night-light on and put a blanket in the crib before she goes to sleep. Those are the essentials." She smiled at Lily, who was sitting quietly on Amy's lap. "Now, you be a good girl for Amy."

Lily made a gurgling noise in her throat as if she was agreeing. Helena smiled and tucked a strand of Lily's hair behind her ear. "If you want anything, you'll have to call Amy instead of Mum. Can you say Amy, Lily?"

Lily pushed her thumb into her mouth and gazed at her mother with a solemn expression.

"We'll be fine," Amy assured her, thinking how nice Helena looked. "You'd better go or you'll be late. Dad's already honked the horn twice."

Helena smoothed a wrinkle out of her black dress, dropped a kiss on Lily's head, and then hurried from the kitchen. "Thanks again," she called over her shoulder.

"Well," said Amy to Lily with a smile. "It looks like it's just you and me."

Lily stared back at her with wide brown eyes that were just like Helena's. Strawberry jam was smeared around the corners of her mouth. "Let's clean you up," Amy said as she wiped it away. She breathed a sigh of relief when Lily didn't object.

"Now, then, little half sister," Amy went on. "How about some playtime and then a bedtime story?" She picked Lily up out of the chair and placed her on her hip the way she had seen Helena do.

"Oooh gone," Lily suddenly told her in solemn tones.

"That's right, Oooh's gone away for a while. But she'll be back soon," Amy said brightly as she made her way up the stairs to Lily's nursery.

Helena had decorated the nursery herself. A mural was painted around three of the walls, showing a paddock full of horses grazing. On the fourth wall was a stable with a gray pony's head looking out over the door. Mobiles hung from the ceiling. There was a cuddly collection of soft toys sitting on a couple of shelves, and the rocking chair next to Lily's crib held a stack of colorful picture books.

Amy sat Lily on a blanket on the floor and they spent some time playing with stacking rings and blocks. After a while, Lily began to rub her eyes and fuss, so Amy gently placed her in her crib.

She covered Lily with a blanket and selected a picture book. For the whole time that Amy turned the pages and talked about the pictures, she was aware that Lily hardly took her eyes off her. When Amy finally closed the book and smiled, Lily smiled back. "Oooh," she said quietly.

"No, not Oooh. Amy. Time to go to sleep now, Lily," Amy told her. She sighed as she clicked on Lily's night-light, switched off the main light, and left the room. She supposed she should be grateful that Lily had been good for her, but their time together seemed to pass so quickly, and it was clear that she still hadn't formed the same kind of bond with her little sister as Lou had.

Amy wandered down to the kitchen and washed Lily's dishes. Then she decided to make herself a cup of coffee. She plugged the coffee machine into the wall and flicked on the switch. The room was instantly plunged into darkness. Amy looked around, but there weren't lights in the next room either. *The fuse must have blown*, Amy thought, wondering where she'd find the breaker box.

Suddenly, a frightened scream sounded from upstairs.

Chapter Ten

❧

"I'm coming, Lily, hang on," Amy called as she felt her way through the darkness. She guessed that Lily's night-light must have been on the same circuit as the kitchen lights. Her hands brushed against rough stone and she knew she must be going through the arch that led from the kitchen into the living room. She used the bookshelf and then the back of the sofa to guide herself to the bottom of the stairs. All the time, she called reassuringly to Lily.

Once she was in the nursery she quickly made her way to the crib and grabbed hold of Lily. She swung her sister up into her arms and rocked her gently until her crying stopped. A sudden surge of protectiveness took her by surprise.

"It's all right," she soothed.

"Amee," Lily hiccuped.

Amy felt her heart skip. "Yes, Lily, Amy's here. I've got you. You're going to be fine now."

Holding Lily close, Amy made her way from the nursery to Tim and Helena's bedroom. She flipped the switch and the lights came on. Amy was relieved they were on a different circuit. Amy set Lily down on the bed and then looked around. She remembered seeing a flashlight somewhere in the room and figured she could use that to find the breaker box downstairs. She soon spotted it on the mantelpiece and picked it up.

She turned back to Lily and felt a tug of emotion at the sight of her sister's tearstained face.

"There, now, the lights work in here. That's better, isn't it?" she said cheerfully to Lily.

"Amee," said Lily again, and she held her arms up, clearly wanting the security of her sister's arms.

🐚

Amy quickly located the breaker box under the stairs and pushed the circuit breaker back up. Light filled the kitchen and the living room again — Amy assumed Lily's night-light also sprang back to life, but instead of putting Lily back in bed, Amy gathered some of her toys and settled down on the sofa with her. "We've got a lot of catching up to do," she told her sister, who beamed brightly.

Amy spent the next hour playing games with Lily and singing the nursery rhymes that she remembered her own mother singing to her. Eventually, Lily yawned and curled up against Amy, who planted a kiss on her curly hair. "My little sister," she whispered, feeling for the first time in her stay that she could grow accustomed to her new role.

✿

Amy woke up to the sound of voices. Blinking the sleep from her eyes, she looked up to see Helena and Tim standing over her and Lily, who slept peacefully in her lap. "Hi," Amy yawned. "Did you have a nice time?"

"Lovely, thanks," Helena answered. "Wouldn't Lily go to sleep for you?"

Amy told them about the circuit breaker and then offered to put Lily back in her crib. After she had tucked her in, she made her way back down to the living room. Tim's and Helena's voices were coming from the kitchen. She was about to join them but hesitated as she heard her name mentioned. She didn't want to eavesdrop, but it was difficult not to hear as their voices carried clearly through the arch. She heard her father say, "I think that Amy's been a little happier here these last few days, even with Lou away."

"Maybe that's helped," Helena put in. "Maybe Amy felt a little overshadowed by Lou."

"I don't see how," Tim mused, sounding puzzled. "Amy's always been so confident."

"Yes, but she's in a whole new element here," Helena said. "It's not always easy coming to a new place and meeting new people."

Tim sighed. "That's true. I wish I could spend more time with them."

"They understand how busy you are," Helena reassured him. "Besides, this is only their first trip. I hope they'll be back."

Amy began to feel awkward and was just wondering if she should go up to her room when Helena spoke again.

"I just wish I could connect with Amy a little more," Helena went on. "I have a feeling I don't really know her yet. I just want her to understand that I'm here for her," she said, sounding wistful.

"She knows. Just give her a bit more time. This has got to be more difficult for her than for Lou. She was incredibly close to Marion," Tim explained.

Amy decided that she couldn't walk into the kitchen now. Instead, she quietly made her way up to her bedroom. As she lay down on the bed and rested her head on her arms, Amy felt as if things were in a much better place. The events of the night had proven that she could be a big sister to Lily. She realized now that that kind of relationship requires the same as any other: time. And Helena's words had opened her eyes, too. She was finally able to see her stepmother's kindness and openness. She felt bad for keeping her at a distance for so long.

Amy also felt a special understanding between herself and her father. He had a sense of what she was going through, but had given her space to sort out her emotions. She wished she had realized what everyone had been feeling. If so, she would not have felt isolated, but welcomed — and loved.

There was only one thing still troubling Amy: the fact that her father didn't have a photo of her on his desk along with the ones of Lou and Lily. Even as she thought about it, Amy felt her stomach churn a little. She closed her eyes and tried to push it to the back of her mind, determined to concentrate instead on all the positive things that had happened recently.

❧

Amy spent the next few days working with Mistral and Spirit and going for rides with Emma. She took Mistral for her first trail ride, with Emma on Spirit, and was thrilled at how much the big black horse was starting to enjoy being ridden. Each morning, when Amy came onto the yard, Mistral would be looking over her door and would call gently the moment she appeared.

Amy's relationship with Lily was growing stronger

every day, and she made a point of spending an hour with her, and either Helena or Tim, each afternoon before tea.

The night before Lou was due to come back, Amy was in the kitchen rolling out Play-Doh for Lily. She looked across at Helena, who was looking up a recipe, and decided to share the last worry about Spirit that was on her mind. "It doesn't matter how much I ride Spirit, or how many hours I spend doing T-touch on him, he still doesn't respond to me the way he did to you," she told her.

"I'm sorry, Amy, I just don't know what else to suggest." Helena frowned. "He's such a hard horse to figure out. I still feel so guilty that I disturbed your workout the other day. It was so upsetting to see, and I keep on thinking that I set back your progress."

"No, you shouldn't worry. Spirit was fine the next day," Amy reassured her. "I have been doing some thinking though, and I've come up with an idea that I want to run past you."

Helena turned to open the fridge and Amy noticed how pleased she looked.

"Do you remember when you told me about the time that you spent the night in Spirit's stall?" Amy continued.

Helena faced her, juggling an armful of lettuce, mayonnaise, and eggs. "Yes, it was when he had colic." She nodded.

"Well, I know it's a long shot, but I thought that if I spent the night with Spirit, it might make him bond with me a little more. I know that the reason he formed such a strong link with you was because you helped him through his illness. But I'm hoping that if I spent a similar stretch of time with him, it might erase some of the emotional dependence he has on you."

Helena became quiet for a while as she thought about it. "I agree it might be a long shot, but I can't see how it would do any harm," she said slowly.

"I thought I'd do it tonight," Amy told her.

"Well, I'll pack you a blanket and a thermos," Helena promised. "And some cookies."

Amy found a teething ring and gave it to Lily to suck on. Lily took it and smiled at her before banging it on the tray of her high chair. Amy forgot all about her worries concerning Spirit as she laughed at her little sister and thought how much she enjoyed being in her company.

❧

Amy heaped a pile of fresh straw in one corner of Spirit's stall and spread her blanket over it. The box was warm and softly lit, and Amy thought how easy it would be to fall asleep.

She spent the first hour of the evening giving Spirit a thorough grooming. Spirit stood with his eyes half shut, resting his hind leg. By the time she had finished, Spirit's coat gleamed and his mane and tail were like silk. Amy proceeded to crumble loose lavender powder into his coat and brush it through to encourage him to relax, just as she had shown Emma with Caspian. Finally, she massaged Spirit, moving in slow circles until her arms and fingers ached so much she had to stop.

Spirit let out a contented sigh as Amy settled herself on her bed of straw. She figured it must be the middle of the night as she let out a wide yawn. To keep herself from falling asleep, she began to softly sing old remembered rhymes from her childhood. *Why not?* she thought. *It helped me bond with Lily.*

As she sang, she began to remember the special times she had shared with her mother. Lately, Amy had often thought about the times she would *miss* sharing with her mom. And she had lingered over the fact that her father hadn't been there for her childhood. But now she was realizing that she had had something special that Lou had missed out on — she had been with her mother for all her childhood years. And more than that, her mother had given her a gift — the gift of understanding and healing horses. And in working with horses, Amy knew she had also been able to help many people. Amy felt lucky, knowing how much she had gained from her mother. She would always cherish that — and, while that friendship would always be close to her heart, she knew she could reach out to build new relationships, too.

❧

Amy woke up to the tickle of hot breath on her face and, as she sleepily opened her eyes, she found Spirit nosing her with his muzzle. She pushed him away gently as she sat up and stretched. Judging by the daylight streaming in through the cracks in the door, it was early morning. She got up and began to work her way through her stable chores. Soon she was joined by Emma.

"You look bushed," Emma observed, seeing Amy's tired expression.

"I've felt more awake," Amy admitted with a rueful smile.

"Listen, why don't you let me finish up here while you go and catch up on some sleep?" Emma offered, picking straw out of Amy's hair.

"Thanks," Amy said gratefully. "I just need a quick nap, and then I want to work Spirit."

"Do you think spending the night with him worked?" Emma asked interestedly.

"I hope so," Amy said, yawning as she headed slowly toward the house. *Even if it hasn't,* she thought, *it's done something for me, anyway.* She trudged up the slope, thinking happily of early mornings working at her mother's side.

❧

There was no one up as Amy entered the house and, in no time at all, she was crawling under her comforter. She closed her eyes, promising herself that she would sleep for just an hour. But she slipped into a deep, dreamless sleep until she was woken hours later.

"Wake up, sleepyhead," said a familiar voice.

Amy groaned, thinking she had slept late and would have to rush to catch the school bus. "I'm coming," she mumbled, and then heard her sister laugh.

"I was thinking you'd be waiting outside with a welcome party for me!" Lou declared.

"What?" Amy sat up, looked into Lou's tanned face, and suddenly realized where she was. "You're back!" she exclaimed, hugging her. "Did you have a good time?"

"I had a fantastic time," Lou admitted, a slightly devious smile playing on her lips.

"Good," Amy said, and smiled back. But her sister's smile only grew wider. Amy was puzzled by the expression on her sister's face. Her blue eyes were sparkling brightly, and Amy instinctively felt that Lou had some kind of secret.

"What's going on?" Amy asked curiously. She tried to

look serious, but the happiness radiating from Lou was infectious, and she soon found herself grinning, although she didn't know why.

Before Lou could answer, Amy's attention was attracted by the sunlight glinting off her sister's hand. "Lou," she said slowly, "am I seeing things, or is that a diamond ring you're wearing?"

"You're not, and it is," Lou laughed happily.

Amy felt a great surge of exhilaration. "You and Scott are engaged!"

Lou nodded. "I can hardly believe it myself! Things have been going really well for us — and I knew that he wanted this time away to be special. But I never dreamed of a proposal." Her cheeks turned pink as Amy stared at her, lost for words.

"Tell me how he proposed," Amy said finally. "I want every single detail."

Lou hugged her arms around herself and settled more comfortably on the bed. "Scott wanted to go on an early hike one morning, so we got up when it was still dark. We drove to a secluded spot, and Scott got out and led the way to the crest of a nearby hill. It seemed like he was in a hurry, so I was rushing after him. But when he got to the top, he just turned around and pointed. In the distance, we could see the silhouette of Ayers Rock. We watched as the sky began to lighten. And, just as the first rays of sunlight appeared over the horizon, he asked me to marry him. Then he produced this fabulous champagne picnic from his backpack, and we just sat there and watched the rest of the sunrise." Her voice was soft. "I'll never forget it. It was so beautiful."

"Oh, Lou, I'm so happy for you!" Amy exclaimed excitedly. She felt real joy inside her, and her eyes filled with tears as she hugged her sister.

Lou hugged her back. "Enough about me, what about you? How've you gotten along without me?" she asked, giving Amy a concerned gaze.

"Everything's turning out really well," Amy assured her. She told her all that had happened since she and Scott had been away.

"If I'd known how good this trip was going to be for us, I'd have suggested it six months ago!" Lou laughed.

Amy suddenly glanced at her watch. "It's one o'clock!" she exclaimed. "I've slept for hours."

"Well, you obviously needed it," Lou said practically. "Helena said you were awake for most of the night in Spirit's box."

"Well, that's the best news I've ever been woken up with, anyway," Amy said as she swung her legs off the bed. "You do realize we'll have to have a double celebration now? One here and one at home. Talk about forward planning on Scott's part!" She grabbed her clothes. "Can you do me a favor?" Amy asked as she pulled on her clothes. "I've sort of made some plans myself today.

Do you think you could get Helena down to the schooling ring in about half an hour?"

"Sure." Lou raised her eyebrows with curiosity. "Am I allowed in on the plan?"

"Better if you come with her and you'll get to see it in action," Amy called over her shoulder as she hurried downstairs.

⁖

Amy had memorized the dressage test that she had watched Helena ride on Spirit in the video. As she rode Spirit into the arena for a warm-up, she smoothed his neck. "Come on, boy, don't tell me that last night was for nothing," she murmured as she shortened her reins and asked for a turn on the forehand. Spirit executed it perfectly, but what was more, Amy got the distinct feeling that he wasn't just obeying a command from her, but was working as her partner.

She trotted and cantered him and there was no mistaking a sudden eagerness in his performance that she had never felt before. Gone were the almost lethargic movements. Spirit's paces were proud and elevated — he made Amy feel as if she were floating on air. His ear constantly flickered back to listen to her voice. His whole attention was focused on her, and she could almost hear him asking, *What next?*

But she knew that there was one crucial test that

would prove whether she had been successful with Spirit. She glanced at her watch and then in the direction of the ranch, and her heart beat faster when she saw Tim, Helena, Lou, and Scott coming down the path.

Spirit had noticed them, too, and he called out to Helena as she leaned against the fence. A frown of uncertainty crossed Helena's face, but Amy caught her father's eye and he nodded, as if to say he knew exactly what she was doing and he approved.

"OK, boy, don't let me down now," Amy said under her breath as she directed Spirit away from the fence and into the center of the arena. She halted in the middle and took a deep breath before putting Spirit into the first movement of the dressage test.

From the moment Spirit picked up his lead, Amy felt the difference in him. There was a channel of communication between them that simply hadn't existed before. He carried out the twenty-meter circles and three-looped serpentines in floating, elevated movements, all the while listening to her requests with his ear flicking back to the sound of her voice. When Amy finally halted, she felt a flood of happiness. For the first time, Spirit wasn't regarding her as a passenger but as a partner he respected and trusted.

Next, Amy rode into the adjacent arena that contained a course of twelve jumps. Remembering the last time she had jumped Spirit with Helena watching, she felt a little wary, but this time he wasn't distracted. As she finished the course, soaring over an in-and-out combination, Amy knew she had participated in developing a horse that could well be a future champion. He had a soul that reminded her of only one other horse she had ever ridden — Pegasus. As her eyes sought out her father's, she knew by his stunned expression that he could see it, too.

He made his way across the ring to her and reached up to place his hands over hers. "I've never seen you look more like your mother than when you were riding just now," he said softly. "Watching you brought back so many memories for me."

Amy felt her throat constrict and her eyes fill with tears.

"It's amazing. My memory of her will never fade while I have you. You have her spirit," Tim finished, his voice husky but warm.

&

On their final day at the ranch, Amy, Lou, and Tim went riding together. Lou stroked Mistral's neck as they walked three abreast along a wide path. "I just can't get over the change in her," she enthused.

"Just as I can't get over the change in you," Tim smiled. "I was so disappointed that we didn't get to ride together when I visited Heartland."

Lou grinned. "I was, too. It's taken me a long time to really have confidence around horses again. Thank goodness Amy didn't give up on me."

"Of course I wouldn't!" Amy replied. "But it was all you in the end."

"You deserve some credit," Lou insisted. "You've always encouraged me and guided me and never made me do more than I was ready for."

"Sounds like the way you treat your horses," Tim smiled. "Speaking of which, I'd like for Emma to train the rest of the staff in your methods, Amy."

"Really?" Amy felt her heart skip with pleasure.

Tim nodded. "I've been so impressed with the results you've achieved here that it's convinced me it's the way forward with all my youngsters. If you can keep in contact with Emma — and maybe send her over some of your notes — it would be very helpful."

"Of course," Amy agreed happily. "I think she'll be great." She and Emma had already promised to keep in touch. Emma was going to be riding Spirit in a dressage competition in a couple of weeks, and Amy wanted to hear how everything went. The girls had formed a bond that was growing stronger daily, and Amy was excited to have an official reason to keep in contact.

Tim glanced at his watch. "We'd better head home," he said reluctantly, "or else Helena will send out a hunting party. After all, the barbecue can't start until we get back — not while I've got two of the three guests of honor!"

❧

At the farewell meal that evening, Amy looked around at the same crowd that had gathered on her first evening at the ranch and reflected on how much had changed since then.

She felt a wonderful sense of fulfillment flood through her. She had learned a good deal about herself on this vacation, but she'd gained a better sense of understanding others. Even though Amy knew she would miss her new friends and family, she looked forward to getting home and seeing everyone at Heartland again. She had missed them all so much, especially Ty. A soft smile touched her lips as she thought of Ty and how support-ive he'd been. He had given her honest advice, even though he knew it might be hard for her to hear. With-out his guidance, Amy might not have learned that she wasn't confined to being who she was at Heartland. Ty had convinced her that she could be something more.

Amy glanced up at the sound of a twig snapping on the ground. "Hey," Tim smiled down at her. "Mind if I join you?"

Amy scooted over on the bench. "I was just thinking how lucky I am to have such a wonderful family and friends," she admitted. "I sometimes lose sight of that when I get wrapped up in my work."

Tim looked thoughtful. "I know what you mean," he replied. "There's always so much to do that sometimes it's the people you love who end up missing out." He paused, looking into Amy's eyes. "I'm sorry I haven't been able to spend as much time with you and Lou as I would have liked. I'm also sorry if it's been hard for you. It's a lot to adjust to."

"I did feel a little left out at first," Amy confessed. "But I think that was my fault. It just took me a little time to figure out where I fit in, but now it all makes sense. I'm part of your family."

Tim slowly turned to Amy, and she instinctively reached out and took his hand. "We've had a wonderful time here," she told him. She hesitated, thinking about the photo of herself that had been missing from her father's desk. Spending this time with him, and coming to realize how much he cared for her, she couldn't quite believe that her father would purposefully *not* include her photo alongside Lily's and Lou's. Amy reasoned that it was more likely that her father simply didn't *have* a photograph of her to display. Things were going so well, she felt that now might be a good time to remedy that.

"You know what would make our stay even more special?" she said with a smile. "If we took a picture to help us remember our first time all together."

"That's a great idea," Tim said, squeezing Amy's hand. "What made you think of it?" he asked.

"Well, when I was in your office, I couldn't help but notice that you don't have any photos of me," Amy said. "And I thought you might like to have one."

"I'd love one," Tim said, a brief look of confusion crossing his face. "But I *do* have a photo of you in my office, Amy. You're right next to Lily — the one where you're asleep, holding your teddy bear. Didn't you recognize yourself?" he asked, smiling.

"No," Amy gasped, feeling surprised, delighted, and embarrassed all at once. Her cheeks burned. "I thought maybe you didn't *want* to have a photo of me when I was little. I mean, you really didn't see me much after I was three."

Tim suddenly wrapped her up in a fierce hug. "Amy, I hope you know by now how hard that was for me. I'm sorry I missed those years, and I thought of you every day. I'm so glad we have a chance to make up for it."

Amy nodded against his chest. It was wonderful to hear, even though she realized she had always known it deep down inside. "Thank you so much, Daddy," she said in a muffled voice.

Tim gave her a final squeeze before releasing her. "I'll miss you. But it won't be long before we're together again — at Lou and Scott's wedding!" His eyes crinkled at the corners as his face lit up.

Amy nodded happily. She felt a surge of joy as she considered the times ahead, with the people she loved.

"Now what do you say we go rustle up Lou, Lily, Helena, and Scott for that photo?" Tim said. "I'll just run and grab my camera." He rushed off.

Amy waited until he returned with his camera. Holding hands, Amy and her father made their way back to where the rest of the family gathered.

"Attention, everyone!" Tim called. "Amy had the brilliant suggestion of all of us taking a big family photo before she and Lou head off."

Everyone murmured their appreciation at the idea, and Lou gave Amy a special smile as the family members started to gather.

"Let's pose by the front porch," Helena suggested.

Amy turned to Emma, who was standing nearby. "Would you mind taking it?" she asked her new friend.

"Of course not!" Emma laughed. Tim handed her the camera, and joined the group at the front porch. He wrapped his arm around Amy, so she was comfortably sandwiched between him and Lou, who was holding Lily. Just before Emma snapped the photo, Amy turned and looked at the smiling faces around her. *You can't buy riches like these,* she thought contentedly. *Love is a gift — and it heals us all.*